CLONE
CLONE

Jordan's family was on the hit list of every animal rights group on Earth. Peaceful protests, arson attacks, red paint, abusive messages, loud insults and parcel bombs were everyday dangers for the son of a leading biologist whose job involved cloning animals. Jordan resented the impact that his father's career was having on his own life. He wished that his dad, like his mum, had become a librarian. No one tried to destroy librarians or their sons. No one called them bastards. The sons of librarians did not have to take precautions against kidnapping, didn't have to watch out for firebombs, didn't have to dodge reporters and their persistent probing.

On placards, in hate mail, on the brickwork of his home, on the walls surrounding Patrick's company, Jordan had seen his dad called SCUM, ANIMAL ABUSER, FILTH, TORTURER, and a whole lot more, always in capitals. YOU ARE NOT GOD! At least that meant Jordan wasn't the son of God. Thank God for that. Jordan didn't fancy being Jesus but he didn't fancy being the son of SCUM either.

More Scholastic titles by Malcolm Rose:

The Lawless & Tilley series

The Malcolm Rose Point Crime Collection

The Alibi
Breathing Fear
Concrete Evidence
Flying Upside Down
The Highest Form of Killing
The Smoking Gun
Bloodline

Tunnel Vision
(Winner of the Angus Book Award 1997)

Plague
(Winner of the Angus Book Award 2001 & the Lancashire
Children's Book of the Year Award 2001)

Point

CLONE

MALCOLM ROSE

SCHOLASTIC

Scholastic Children's Books,
Commonwealth House, 1-19 New Oxford Street,
London, WC1A 1NU, UK
A division of Scholastic Ltd
London ~ New York ~ Toronto ~ Sydney ~ Auckland
Mexico City ~ New Delhi ~ Hong Kong

First published in the UK by Scholastic Ltd, 2002

Copyright © Malcolm Rose, 2002

ISBN 0 439 98164 6

Printed and bound in Great Britain by Cox & Wyman Ltd, Reading, Berkshire

1 2 3 4 5 6 7 8 9 10

The right of Malcolm Rose to be identified as the author of this work has been asserted by him
in accordance with the Copyright, Designs and Patents Act, 1988.

For Mum and Dad

With thanks to Kirsty Turrell

Some day we will realize that the prime duty, the inescapable duty, of the good citizen of the right type is to leave his or her blood behind him in the world, and that we have no business to permit the perpetuation of citizens of the wrong type.

Theodore Roosevelt, President of the United States of America, 1901–9.

We plan to transfer the first cloned embryo at the beginning of 2002, so at the end of 2002, the first cloned human baby will be born.

Panayiotis Zavos, Andrology Institute of America, 2001.

It's not so much a question of cloning but freedom of science. Cloning is good.

Raël, author of Yes to Human Cloning, 2002.

PROLOGUE
PROLOGUE

The hooded woman looked about eighty years old but she was barely fifty. A lifetime in the underground had taken its toll. A lifetime of illness had taken its toll. Her back bent, Zadie moved painfully slowly along the frozen track, towards the AFC depot. Dressed in rags and filthy furs against the chill, squinting against the harsh daylight, grim determination was written across her decaying face. Her head permanently bowed by skeletal deformity, she could see only the ground for a few metres ahead. The sunshine reflected up from the snow and ice, blinding her already weak eyes through their narrow slits.

Frail, she stopped to regain her breath and ease the cramp. To look ahead, to see how far she still had to drag herself, she leaned back from the waist. Zadie's waist was one of the few parts of her body that remained supple. The ineffective sun and icy wind stung her face and the hood fell back from her head. Her unruly mass of grey hair was alive with lice. She looked like a twisted scarecrow. Her left arm was fixed into position, crooked across her sunken belly. With her good right arm, she pulled the hood back over her head and held on to it. Her long sigh was whisked away by the breeze.

In front of her lay the ugly industrial complex of the Anti-Freeze Corporation, the storage tanks and two grounded aircraft. To the right, parallel to the track, two lines of blue spotlights marked the AFC's runway. Beyond it, there was nothing but a blinding whiteness. Behind her and to her left were the outskirts of the sprawling city. Westford had been her home but, as she took one last look at the place, she felt nothing in her heart. There was no emotional response, no fondness. Somewhere in the city's underground there were a few mutes she'd miss but the brightly painted houses, the city's freeways, the enormous snow-capped fertility clinic, the newly built nuclear fusion power station, the Leisure Dome and Protected Park meant nothing to her. Like the rest of the mutes, she was excluded from all of these things. Leaning forward into her natural curve, Zadie resumed her weary slog towards the AFC unit.

All over the developed world, mutes like Zadie were trudging to their own particular targets: reservoirs, farms that sprayed pesticides from aircraft, food distribution centres, canning factories, fertility clinics. Zadie was comforted by the fact that she was not the only one. If she had been acting alone, she might have harboured some doubt. But, no. She was a small part of a big picture. And she had a promise to keep, a duty to fulfil. She was convinced that what she was about to do was right. There was no humanity in the world, only human beings, and the mutes were making sure that human beings would soon follow humanity into history.

It was AFC's job to keep open the major arterial routes and airports, and to assist any viable agriculture. The corporation's aeroplanes flew non-stop sorties against the enemy:

ice. They sprayed anti-freeze solution on to Priority 1 sites like runways, railways, motorways, and the few remaining farms in the south where barley had been genetically modified to grow in the cold and to thrive on melted ice.

Drained, Zadie sank to the ground, out of the wind and blinding sunlight, her back propped against the thick plastic wall of the anti-freeze tank. For a few minutes, she could do nothing but gasp down air, stingingly cold, past her overgrown tongue and into her aching lungs. Then, before iciness froze her to the spot, she took the vial out from under the layers of fur. For a moment she held it in her gloved hand like an elderly nun clutching a crucifix in the moment before death. The fluid inside the vial looked like pure water but it wasn't. In the underground, it had become known as the agent of retribution. It was a strong solution of a bacterium and its toxin, and it would not freeze even in this weather. It didn't need the faint warmth of Zadie's body to stay liquid. The bacteria that caused botulism were far too small to be seen with the naked eye, yet two hundred grams of the toxin it produced would kill every one of the four billion human beings on the planet.

Around the globe there had been many more people, of course. Eight billion of them. Scientists said the world could feed them all and it did briefly. But that was before floods, drought or ice claimed large tracts of land. And it was before the storms. The heavily inhabited planet ran short of viable agricultural land, food and clean water. Fields became too hot, too cold, too dry, too wet, or too degraded to grow natural crops. Global warming allowed no middle ground; it brought only extremes. In the grip of starvation, disease and homelessness, the human population plummeted. And a lot of men became as barren as the expanding deserts. Like fields turning to wasteland and refusing seed, more and more men could not father babies. The birth rate plummeted as well. Still, revenge was so much easier in an exhausted world.

Maybe it would have been different if Zadie had been able to have a child. Maybe she would have seen the world differently then. But the baby hadn't come. No matter how many men she'd tried, her life remained unfulfilled. Now, no child would mourn her passing. Zadie's working right hand offered the glass vial to her fixed left hand as if it were a vice. She gripped the flask in her gloved bony fist, mumbled a quiet prayer, and then broke the seal with her right hand. Clamping her forefinger over the small hole and returning the vial to her right hand, she scrambled back on to her feet.

All of a sudden, she shed forty years. She could hear the sounds of the young norms when she was little, throwing snowballs playfully at each other. Zadie didn't join in, couldn't join in. Silently, she stayed in the doorway of the underground and watched at a distance. A boy called David had his arm twisted behind his head, madly trying to extract a snowball from the back of his neck. "Oh, Catriona," he exclaimed. "You're horrid!" But he didn't mean it. He was laughing. The girl who had sneaked up behind him and dropped the icy surprise down his neck was also having fun. But her laugh might have had a malicious edge. What struck Zadie most was Catriona's appearance. She was gorgeous. Absolutely gorgeous. Utterly perfect. She could rough up any boy she wanted because they'd always come back for more. Catriona was everything Zadie wanted to be but wasn't. Zadie doubted that the good-looking norms saw her at all. They certainly tried not to see her but, if they did, they ignored her. Even as a child, she wasn't a pretty sight.

Now old and feeble, she was not going to be invisible any more. This time, she was joining in. With one final effort, she turned, pulled back her right arm and hurled the vial high over the side of the storage tank. The wind obliterated the sound of it landing on top, but in her imagination she saw the flask rolling to the lowest point, the liquid dripping slowly from the opening, leaking into the antifreeze that would soon be sprayed across the country and onto the southern farms that would grow tomorrow's crops.

1

To the right of the cherry tree, the night air was cut to ribbons. Maynard Litzoff stepped out as if slipping through a doorway draped with clear plastic strips. Pushing aside the transparent curtain, Maynard glanced around the garden. It was a warm, still night in Westford. Not a sign of snow. It felt incredibly warm. He was overdressed. He hesitated for a moment but seemed satisfied that no one had witnessed his arrival. Leaving behind the frozen wastes, the dead and the dying, he stepped nervously through. Standing on the lush lawn, he looked down at his watch where the red digits glowed faintly. His temperature was more or less normal. His pulse was galloping but that was expected. He felt fine. And it was the right time – the middle of the night. He took a deep breath.

He yanked off his gloves, pushed them into a pocket of his padded coat and crept silently towards the back door. As soon as he got near to the house, though, he was engulfed unexpectedly in light. He froze for several seconds. Then he moved to the side, trying to evade the glare, but another spotlight came on and caught him. Next, he heard a shout. It was a young male voice, rather like his own. "What are you doing? What's going on?" Maynard turned and fled back towards his own doorway.

*

Jordan Finch was singing a quiet song under his breath as he wandered back home, a little dizzy. Pleasantly light-headed, he slurred the words of the song. He'd told his mum and dad he'd be back by 12.30 but . . . someone had heard about a house party and, once the pub had closed, all of his mates had decided it was too good an opportunity to miss. When they got there, it turned out to be awash with girls, good music, drink and . . . well, the next time Jordan checked his watch, it was two o'clock.

At the start of the year, his mum had insisted that he should promise always to tell her where he was going and who with, always to keep in touch, always to get back home at the agreed time. She'd told him how important it was, particularly with his dad doing what his dad did. But by April the resolution had gone the way of most New Year resolutions. It wasn't that Jordan had forgotten, that he hadn't understood the importance of keeping his word, that he'd underestimated the danger, especially with his dad doing what his dad did. It was just that things happening in Jordan's life seemed far more important than things happening in his parents' lives. Jordan didn't want his time to be dictated by his dad's job. That wouldn't be fair. To Jordan, going to a late-night party was much more than going to a party: it was defiance against Patrick Finch.

A car prowled along the road and a cat, its eyes glistening, scampered out of the way and up a drive. The car passed and once again only the orange streetlamps kept the night at bay. Then, abruptly, there was another light. Through the hedge, at the back of his own house, one of the spotlights had come on. Jordan was finely tuned to disturbances. Over the years, he'd been trained to be suspicious about strange noises, objects placed near the house or that had been moved, anything out of the ordinary. An ingrained nervousness made him alert at all times. Even in his woozy state, he darted round to the back of the house. A boy, about the same age as himself, had triggered a couple of security lamps and was trapped in the blaze, dithering. He was wearing enough clothing to undertake an arctic expedition. Immediately, Jordan knew why. Anonymous demonstrators laboured under acres of clothing to protect their identities against prying closed-circuit television cameras. He shouted, "What are you doing? What's going on?"

At once, the boy took off, just like the cat. He flew towards the cherry tree, dived towards the hedge and then pulled up, puzzled. The intruder's reaction reminded Jordan of someone who had not realized that he had reached the top of some stairs, tried to take another step, and was surprised to find himself stumbling. He reached out a hand, grabbed a part of a bush to steady himself, hesitated, and then burst right through the hedge, uttering a cry before spilling out on to the pavement beyond.

Jordan winced. He knew from painful experience that the twiggy thorny hedge could gash skin right through the heaviest clothing. He smiled and, on behalf of the shadowy intruder, he murmured, "Ouch!" Right now, that boy's hands, wrists and face would be a mass of scratches. Serves him right, though.

Jordan adjusted the glasses on his nose. He wasn't going to attempt a chase. He wasn't in a fit state for a pursuit and it would be far too risky anyway. The boy might be one of those who armed himself with much more than a can of spray paint. Above Jordan, the light of the back bedroom came on and Jordan's dad appeared at the window. His parents were light sleepers, also finely tuned to night-time sounds. Besides, his mum always claimed that she never slept until she heard him come safely home.

By the time that Jordan got round to the front door, his anxious dad was there in his dressing gown, ready to give Jordan a dressing down, and his mum was already on the phone.

Jordan was grateful when the police officers arrived. He'd heard enough of his parents' nocturnal lecture on responsibility and welcomed the light relief of being interviewed by the police instead. Not that he had anything significant to report. The video pictures stored on the family's computer gave the officers a much better description than a slightly drunk Jordan could manage.

One police officer looked up from the overdressed youth on the monitor. "I don't need to tell you what this is."

Gwen Finch nodded. "I know."

"Looks like Jordan interrupted him before he could do anything."

Jordan knew exactly what was on their minds. The police and his parents had one word for people like this boy: terrorists. Jordan had another. He called them protesters. Whatever their label, they had become an integral and intrusive part of Jordan's life. Everything had to be geared to them, terrorists or protesters. Every letter, padded envelope and parcel posted to the house had to be checked by the bomb squad, a sniffer dog, an X-ray machine and a variety of chemical detectors before it got anywhere near their letter box. Mail for any of his dad's work premises in England or overseas was intercepted and monitored even more thoroughly. Every time Jordan went out, he had to report his whereabouts at regular intervals. And he was told never to trust anyone who tried to befriend him. Every time the Finches used the car, they had to scan underneath for suspect packages. In a year or two, when Jordan started to drive himself, he'd have to get his own mirror on a pole. Jordan wondered if bomb spotting would form part of a driving test designed especially for him. The household dustbin had to be kept locked away in case anyone dropped an incendiary device into it. The house was riddled with cameras. Jordan couldn't kiss a girl without images of the encounter appearing on a computer screen, stored for ever on a CD-ROM.

It was all routine for a family on the hit list of every animal rights group on Earth. Peaceful protests, arson attacks, red paint, abusive messages, loud insults and parcel bombs were everyday dangers for the son of a leading biologist whose job involved cloning animals. Jordan resented the impact that his father's career was having on his own life. He wished that his dad, like his mum, had become a librarian. No one tried to destroy librarians or their sons. No one called them bastards. The sons of librarians did not have to take precautions against kidnapping, didn't have to watch out for firebombs, didn't have to dodge reporters and their persistent probing.

Jordan's best friend had an MP for a father and everyone thought that was bad enough. Politicians had only recently crawled out of the swamp, but they were still several rungs higher on the evolutionary scale than Jordan's dad. On placards, in hate mail, on the brickwork of his home, on the walls surrounding Patrick's company, Jordan had seen his dad called SCUM, ANIMAL ABUSER, FILTH, TORTURER, and a whole lot more, always in capitals. YOU ARE NOT GOD! At least that meant Jordan wasn't the son of God. Thank God for that. Jordan didn't fancy being Jesus but he didn't fancy being the son of SCUM either.

The sergeant took a copy of the video recording so he could try to identify the boy by entering his image into a facial recognition system. For years, the police had been turning up at every protest and demonstration with video recorders. They had amassed a huge database of extremists. Now, the police computer knew every troublemaker by the precise dimensions of the head, the length and thickness of the lips, the distance between the eyes, skin colour, the position of the ears, and the size of the nose.

"You could get a DNA sample off the bush as well," Jordan added. "He must have scratched himself so there'll be traces of blood."

For a moment, the police officer looked surprised at Jordan's knowledge.

"Science runs in the family," said Gwen.

The police officer nodded. "We'll get forensics in once we've got daylight."

"Let's hope it doesn't rain," Patrick remarked.

Their duty done, the officers left and, just before dawn, Jordan went upstairs to get a few hours of restless sleep.

*

A hangover was a dark bottomless pit. The next morning, Jordan was dangling over the abyss, clinging to its edge by his fingertips, not quite tumbling down uncontrollably. His head felt vaguely detached but not unbearable. He felt sick but not in imminent danger of needing to sprint to the bathroom. When he was called down into the garden, he could respond without the world tipping alarmingly upside down as long as he avoided sudden movements.

Outside, under Jordan's guidance, a couple of forensic scientists swabbed the hedge for blood samples. They did the job quickly and then hurried away. Jordan got the impression that they had more serious cases to grace with their presence. Head bowed, Jordan let out a long breath and then gulped fresh morning air. When he turned to go inside, a flash caught his eye. Puzzled, he walked towards the hedge, got down gingerly on his hands and knees, waited for the throbbing in his head to subside and then reached under the bush. His fingers contacted a crisp packet and something metallic. Clutching it, Jordan withdrew his hand and found himself holding a digital watch. Standing up again, he wiped the dirt off it. He guessed that a twig must have caught that boy's arm last night and yanked the watch from his wrist. Jordan imagined that he should hand it over to the police but he iked the look of it. Besides, there was nothing to identify its owner.

Curious, Jordan wandered back inside and upstairs, keeping his eye on his find. It wasn't a cheap watch. It doubled as a calculator, calendar, alarm, stopwatch and it seemed to have some monitoring functions that Jordan could not fathom. On the reverse, there seemed to be some sort of sensor that would be in contact with the wearer's skin. Back in his bedroom, Jordan soon discovered that tapping a button on the side of the watch switched between its various modes. The main display showed the correct time and date: 09:27 on 19 April 2002. A second time zone on the watch had also been set to 09:27 on 19 April but the year was hopelessly wrong. It had been entered as 2152. His headache and sickness forgotten, Jordan muttered with a smile, "So you're as good at setting digital watches as you are at breaking and entering."

In Britain, the headquarters of the Finch Private Human Cloning Clinic disguised itself as the Finch Private Fertility Clinic. Out of view of the television cameras, the technicians were breeding the next generation of chimpanzees. Of the one hundred experiments set up, the biologists expected about 96 failures and maybe four successful implants. At least one of those four would probably produce a deformed embryo that would have to be aborted. At least one other would probably miscarry. If a couple of embryos survived until birth, one would probably die soon after, often grotesquely large, its face squashed, definitely defective. If the technicians were lucky, they might get one successful, long-lived and perfectly formed chimp.

Patrick Finch could not expect to stay out of the limelight for long. He sat in the Clinic's meeting room, sipped rosehip tea, and faced a hostile press on live TV. He enjoyed a good argument, he liked justifying himself, as long as he was in control. In this arena, he felt nervous and uncomfortable but he still wore a look of supreme confidence. And integrity. Oozing honesty was the most important thing of all. Throughout the barrage of questions, he reminded himself constantly that what he was doing was right. He was the good guy, a friend to the childless.

Jordan sat at home in front of the television and flinched while the reporters, packed in like sardines, tried to roast his dad in public. Jordan saw in his dad's face the tiny cracks in his bravado as he attempted to read a statement: something about reproductive human cloning defeating male sterility, something about responsible ethical science helping infertile men to have children bearing their own DNA, something about the necessity of studying animal clones. But the journalists had turned up to find out what they wanted to know and not what Patrick Finch thought they ought to know. They jumped up and down as only journalists on heat can. The press conference was headed for chaos.

"Where are you going to clone a baby? It's banned in Britain."

"For the moment, it's effectively banned, yes. But we have offers from six different countries."

"Where?"

"No final decision's been taken yet," Patrick lied.

"When are you going to do it?"

"We expect to produce a human clone within three years."

There was uproar and at least six questions shouted at the same time. Patrick – and anyone watching the broadcast – couldn't make out any of them. "One at a time!" he cried.

"Whose baby will it be?"

"A childless couple where the man has no sperm of his own. We've got several hundred such couples, all desperate for this technology."

15

"What about rich cranks who just want to duplicate themselves?"

"It won't work and it won't happen. We're a clinic providing a service for infertile people in a stable relationship. That's all."

"How much are you charging?" the man from the *Sun* queried.

"A realistic figure."

"How many thousands?"

"That's between the clinic and our clients."

"Give us some names!"

Patrick smiled sweetly and turned towards another reporter.

The BBC's science correspondent asked, "Which creatures have you cloned so far?"

"Mice, cats, sheep, cattle, pigs, goats and chimpanzees."

"What's the failure rate with them?"

Patrick gave a wry smile. "Higher than we would wish."

"Given that, aren't you being incredibly irresponsible to do it with humans?"

"No. We won't have the same number of failures. For one thing, people won't suffer the same gene errors as animals. Anyway, every human embryo we make will be screened using our own proven method before a perfect one is chosen for implantation into the mother. Once flawed embryos are screened out, the chances of a successful pregnancy will be as good as any other artificial fertilization treatment."

"So, you kill ninety-nine per cent of the foetuses and let one live," a brash voice shouted from the back.

"Kill isn't the right word. And neither is foetuses. They're cells, barely visible to the naked eye, not foetuses, and they aren't alive."

"Aren't they?"

Patrick ignored the question, looking again at the woman from the BBC.

Shouting above the hubbub, she said, "As I understand it, you take a cell from an adult, isolate the genes and inject them into an egg taken from the mother after her own genes have been removed."

The tension that Jordan could see in his dad's face suddenly faded. He was on comfortable ground here, dealing with the facts. "Yes. Exactly. We use a tiny pulse of electricity to blend the genes and egg into a single cell. The electricity also convinces the adult genes they're young again. Then, the cell begins to divide and grow. In other words, it becomes an embryo. Eventually, and perfectly normally back in mum's womb, it develops into a foetus."

Jordan smiled to himself. There. By a dictionary definition, not even one of his dad's clones could be called a bastard. It'd be born into a stable relationship with a father; it'd come from a family union of a sort. It was just that a male baby would look the same as its own father. Hardly a bastard. When protesters called Jordan a BASTARD, it was equally inappropriate. He didn't even approve of his dad's work.

At the clinic, Patrick's sense of relief did not last for long.

"How does the kick-start work? How does electricity rejuvenate old genes?"

"We don't know precisely, but it does work. If you're

anything like me, you don't know exactly how your laptop works but you still rely on it."

"Yes. And it crashes pretty regularly."

"As I said," Patrick replied, "our screening procedure will weed out faulty embryos at a very early stage."

The familiar voice from the back boomed, "Ah, it's 'weed out' rather than 'kill'. It's still unacceptably wasteful and plain immoral. That's what people'll say. Are you a religious man, Dr Finch?"

"I have beliefs," Patrick answered. "And I believe in helping couples to have children."

"Does everyone have the right to reproduce?"

"Yes," Patrick answered firmly.

"Isn't infertility God's way of telling a couple they don't?"

At once, Patrick retorted, "Isn't God telling you something when He gave me the ability to clone human beings?"

Another boisterous voice called out, "You're playing God!"

The reporter from the *Sun* yelled, "You're just feathering your own nest, Finch."

"The public's disgusted at the thought of human cloning."

"What you're doing is evil," someone else shouted.

The scientist in Jordan could see his dad's point of view but Jordan the boy was still horrified by it all. Watching his dad face this pack of hungry hounds alone, though, Jordan almost felt sympathy for him. Jordan had always been half-proud, half-ashamed by his father's ability to stand at the crease facing thunderbolts and knock them relentlessly for six. He still remembered a Parents' Evening at school when his dad squared up to Mr Ricketts and insisted that Jordan was taken out of his RE lessons to do something more worthwhile, like extra science. "You don't need God to explain the world," his dad had said, "and there's no evidence He exists."

Mr Ricketts wore a courteous smile. "I've never seen my own skeleton but I know it's there, holding me up. I don't need the evidence of my own eyes. God's the same. I don't need to see Him to know He gives me as much support as my bones."

To a young Jordan, that sounded like a good, clever response. But then Dad lifted his hefty bat. "The day God shows up on an X-ray, I'll ask you to take Jordan back into RE."

On television, the question-and-answer session was threatening to turn into a slanging match. Trying to restore the calm, Patrick said, "I tell you, as soon as the first baby's born, as soon as it cries and feeds like any other baby, as soon as it does baby-like things, we'll all forget how it came into the world. It'll be just another ordinary healthy baby, flesh and blood like the rest of us, loved by its mum and dad, and its different upbringing will make it entirely different from the one parent who provided its genes. Cloning'll become another valuable and unremarkable IVF treatment."

"Will it be born with its parent's memories?"

"No, that's nonsense," Patrick said with disdain. "The only things that're carried over are genes. Each clone goes back to square one. Like any normal baby, it's a blank tape.

19

Physically much the same as its parent – a chip off the old block if you like – but it'll record lots of different things from scratch."

Jordan had heard it all before. His dad had developed that analogy in answer to one of Jordan's own questions. The clones of a single parent, he'd said at home, would be like a box of rewritable compact discs – all the same but they will each store a large, different, fantastic and unique set of experiences. End result? On playback, each one is totally individual. Over family meals – when they happened – Jordan subjected his dad to a grilling that wasn't as heated as this trial by television but, in its way, it was just as demanding.

At the press conference, some rogue demonstrator-cum-terrorist in a balaclava ran in front of Patrick's desk and hurled an egg at him. The microphones picked up a scream of, "Spawn of the devil!" Milking the moment, the cameras zoomed in as Patrick wiped the slush from his face. The protester had transformed a hotchpotch of a press conference into a televisual feast.

Jordan fought hard to suppress a grin. After all, some big bloke in Security was going to lose his job for allowing the demonstrator to get through, for allowing the cameras to see Dr Finch with egg on his face. Even so, it was very funny. Watching the media feeding frenzy, Jordan hoped that none of those reporters would ever be cloned. They were perfectly capable of slagging off his dad in their newspapers and yet he imagined that, if they ever found themselves infertile, they'd be queuing at the door of one of his clinics.

20

Like the journalists, though, Jordan was itching to know who'd be at the head of the queue. Who was going to be first to break the taboo? Would it be a rich patient? Or would Jordan's dad dare to clone himself? It was a long-standing tradition in medicine for the doctor to take the treatment first. It was supposed to say something about confidence in the medical breakthrough. But it wouldn't be that way with cloning. If Patrick Finch cloned himself the press would be on to it like a shot. The mad scientist would get a couple of new labels: SELFISH and ARROGANT. No. Jordan wouldn't get a brother like that. Actually, it wouldn't be a brother anyway. The child would be identical to Patrick so it would be a second father – a miniature dad – or maybe an uncle.

Would Jordan's dad clone his own wife? Possibly. By the time Jordan reached the age of twenty, he could have a brand new baby mother-cum-aunt-cum-sister. Or would Patrick clone Jordan? Perhaps. How would Jordan feel with not just a brother, not just a young twin, but another Jordan? He would no longer be unique. The artificial twin would devalue him. Jordan would feel that, if he were to die, his parents would not be so devastated because they'd got a ready-made replacement in the bank. A forgery.

How did his friends Myleene and Anita feel? They were identical twins, sharing exactly the same genes. Did one twin feel devalued by the other? Jordan doubted it. They seemed to take mischievous delight in being identical twins. At least they used to. Jordan smiled. That playful gene the sisters shared often got them out of trouble. Sometimes it got them into trouble as well.

Just because it was possible to make an endless supply of lookalikes – just because God had given Dr Finch the ability to copy people – Jordan didn't believe it was right. After all, God had made it possible for scientists to make nuclear missiles. That didn't necessarily mean He approved of lighting the blue touch-paper.

On screen, Jordan's dad was retreating from the room, pursued by raised voices.

3

Maynard's right hand clutched his left wrist, barely believing what had happened. Distraught, he kept feeling his sleeve as if his watch would turn up like a key lost at the bottom of a pocket if he rooted around for long enough. For Maynard that watch *was* his key. Without it, he felt naked. Like all modern watches, it monitored his body temperature, metabolism and pulse. Yet, unique among watches, his had one very special additional purpose. Without it, he was stranded.

On top of that, he had messed up a simple mission. Maynard couldn't get back to Finch's house because it was patrolled by police officers. When the spotlights had come on and Jordan Finch had discovered him, the Finch family must have contacted the police. He had been barred from his target and from the place where he'd probably lost his watch. He groaned to himself.

In the damp dreary morning Maynard sat, miserable like a lot of Westford's other homeless people, under the railway bridge. He felt as if he were among mutes for the first time in his life and that made him embarrassed and even more ill at ease. Of course, the characters wrapped in bags and cardboard boxes, huddled over a small fire, dragging on soggy cigarette butts, or simply staring absently into the distance weren't actually mutes. Mutants would emerge

23

only after human cloning began. Even so, to Maynard, they looked as unkempt, imperfect and inferior as mutes. Trying to ignore them, and trying to put the lost watch to the back of his mind for the moment, he read a grubby newspaper that he'd found in the street. It was something called the *Sun*. Splashed over pages two and three was an article on the Finch Private Fertility Clinic. Instead of reporting the facts, or simply reproducing the written information that the clinic had released yesterday, the newspaper let rip under a headline of SCIENCE GONE MAD: HERE COMES THE MASTER RACE. Because the sub-headings were comical – *Finch flies into controversy, Finch counts his chickens* – Maynard didn't know if the article was to be taken seriously or not. It even gave an illustration of the result of cloning perfect sets of genes. On page three there were six identical nude models, *Finch's birds of a feather*, all called Tracey, all 20 years old, all thin, pretty and busty. Maynard didn't understand that either. It would have been more accurate to show six identical babies. And why all female? That didn't make sense at all when so many communities would opt for male babies.

Maynard may have been confused about the newspaper treatment but he was still certain about one thing. Patrick Finch had to be taken very seriously. His declared strategy for human cloning would be a disaster – SCIENCE GONE MAD: HERE COMES THE MASTER RACE – and it had to be averted. That was Maynard's purpose. Maynard had to save not just humanity but human beings as well.

In the newspaper there was also a picture of some people

wearing balaclavas. With their all-over clothing, they looked as if they were adapting to the same chilly weather that Maynard had long since been hardened against. Judging by the report, these shrouded demonstrators came closest to the truth. Their dire warnings and misgivings about cloning struck a chord with Maynard.

The buses and taxis and cars queuing at the junction, waiting for the traffic lights to turn green, blanketed society's underclass with light blue exhaust fumes. The others didn't seem to notice the fug that had settled on them but Maynard coughed over and over again. When two of the outcasts approached him, Maynard tried to put aside his deep-seated prejudice, determined not to judge these people until he knew what they were really like. He had to fight his instincts, though, because every norm was trained to regard mutes as unworthy and degenerate. One of the men was so pathetically short and the other so lanky that they hardly seemed to belong to the same species. Definitely pre-cloning. They didn't have the standard features of perfect human beings. The squat one was muscular, like a bodybuilder in miniature. His soiled woolly hat had *Manchester United* printed across it. Maynard knew Manchester, of course, but he didn't know what Manchester United meant. He assumed it was some sort of political statement.

The man nodded towards Maynard's clothes and said, "Ugly but warm."

"Too warm," Maynard remarked.

Quick to spot an opportunity, the man replied, "Oh yeah? You going to ditch 'em?"

Thinking of the unforgiving weather at home, Maynard shook his head. "No."

The large one, still in his teens, said nothing at all. With his overwhelming size and his silence, he could have been threatening but his face was almost childlike, friendly yet bewildered.

Maynard asked, "I need a television device. Is there one near here?"

"Telly? Here? What's someone like you want a telly for?"

Maynard certainly wasn't going to tell this stranger that, according to the newspaper, Dr Finch was holding a press conference in front of the television cameras today. He shrugged. "I just . . . do."

"You're new around here."

Maynard wasn't sure if the Manchester United man was asking a question or making an observation. "Yes."

"Come on. We'll take you to the shop. Nothin' better to do, like. It's warm and Lights Out likes seeing all the electrical stuff he'll never have." Manchester United looked up at his friend and raised his voice as if he were calling to someone high up on a hillside. "Don't you?"

"Da."

Maynard looked puzzled but joined the men anyway. In height, Maynard neatly filled the gap between them. They led him down Westford's high street, dangerously close to the chugging vehicles, past peculiar shops offering all sorts of goods, some recognizable, some not. Nodding towards the taller man, Maynard asked, "Why do you call him Lights Out?" It seemed rude to talk about Lights Out, rather than talk to him, but it was clearly expected.

"Because when he's in a situation, you know what I mean, he's more than likely to punch someone's lights out. Thwack! I seen him do it. He should be a class boxer but, I mean, he hasn't got no work permit – no sort of papers." He turned to his companion, threw a playful punch at the polluted air and said loudly, "That's right, ain't it, Lights Out?"

In a foreign accent that Maynard couldn't identify, Lights Out said, "I have real name but. . ." He lifted both hands and let them fall again in an expression of hopelessness.

"No papers," Manchester United repeated.

"*Niet*," said Lights Out.

Maynard was perplexed. "*Niet?*"

"He means no."

"*Da.*"

"Yes," Manchester United translated. "Have to see what I can do about that, won't I?"

Abruptly, Maynard stopped by a shop window.

"No tellies in there, man. It's a chemist."

"I know it." Maynard's eye had been caught by a promotional display. *Be prepared for this summer! Factor 25 sunscreen. Extra moisturizing, water resistant, anti-UVA/UVB, photostable, with new skin cell protection system. Three bottles for the price of two.* Maynard coughed and then shook his head. "Let's go."

Manchester United pointed to the other side of the street. "Nearly there." After he'd guided Maynard across the road, he nodded towards the boy's face and said, "Looks like you been dragged through a hedge backwards." He halted by an electrical store and opened the door.

Maynard's hand went to his cheek, decorated with red scabby lines. "No, not backwards." Without offering further explanation, he walked into the shop.

Inside, he was faced with a whole bank of televisions. On one shelf, every screen was showing pictures from the press conference. It looked as if clones of Patrick Finch were preaching from a row of identical pulpits.

"You got a choice," Manchester United said, interrupting Maynard's concentration. "You got your Teletubbies, soap, a chat show, your motors, some boring newsy thing, or a music channel."

Listening to the news broadcast, Maynard pointed to one of the many Patrick Finches.

"You sure got a funny idea of fun."

"Shush."

"Please yourself, like."

Manchester United and Lights Out strolled around the shop while Maynard absorbed Patrick's words and the reactions of the press. Once Lights Out had had his fill of unattainable sandwich toasters, vacuum cleaners, coffee makers, microwave ovens and hi-fis, he returned with his friend to the wall of televisions. On the screens, ten eggs hit ten Patrick Finches full in the face.

"Hey, that's better!" Manchester United cried. "Wallop! Ker-splat! That's more like it. Class act."

Lights Out just watched and laughed raucously.

An assistant came up to them and asked, "Can I help you gentlemen?"

"Help?" Maynard was surprised. "No, thanks. I think that's not. . . I need to do it myself."

"Pardon?"

"We're just off," Manchester United said, ushering his companions towards the door. "They're from . . . abroad, like. English no good."

Thinking about the protester on TV, Maynard walked on autopilot. He was heartened. If the demonstrator had got close enough to throw something at Patrick Finch, Maynard should be able to breach the biologist's security as well. Yet he did not have a missile in mind. He needed something very different.

Alone again on the streets, Maynard used a little of the bizarre money that he'd been given to buy some envelopes, a pad of notepaper and a pen. Red ink seemed right for what he had in mind. He needed only to write a message or an insult on the paper, put it in the envelope along with a sprinkling of virtually invisible hi-tech dust, and deliver it to the Finches' home.

Walking through Westford, Maynard felt vulnerable and overwhelmed. Everything was wrong. He'd been prepared, of course, but even so the ugliness of buildings, vehicles and a lot of the people took him by surprise. Drab concrete and brick was everywhere and the city air was acrid with pollution: the private cars belched a terrifying cocktail of poisonous gases, pungent tobacco smoke lingered everywhere, and it was too hot. And the people were so . . . varied. It wasn't just height. Some were so fat that Maynard feared that he'd bump into them as he walked past. Others were repulsive. Some, even more like mutes than the homeless, could barely move without a stick or walking frame. There was even a cripple, apparently unable to get around at all without a wheelchair. Some of the men were bald. A huge number of people advertised their disability across their faces by wearing spectacles. The old looked ravaged by age rather than dignified by it and the women had lost their youthful figures. Maynard was amazed and shocked by such infirmity. He'd expected diversity and imperfection but not on such a massive scale.

Yet, despite the damaged people and the damaged environment, life here had a certain spice and value. For all their faults, the people were in far higher spirits than the perfect norms of home. Before the botulism – the fatal food poisoning – there was something bland and smug about the wholesome life of a clone. And no amount of science could suddenly make the weather perfect again. The people buzzing around Maynard now – shouting, joking, arguing – were carrying on either not knowing or not caring that their society was careering towards a crossroads for the human race. Those who did know were like Patrick Finch, arrogantly believing that they were in control of nature, or they were dressed in balaclavas, hurling eggs and insults.

The importance of Maynard's task was beyond imagination. He hadn't made the best of starts and he was petrified of failure. Involuntarily, his right hand still strayed to his left wrist, confirming over and over again that his precious watch was not in its place. He couldn't even look after a wristwatch, never mind save the human species from extinction.

He leapt into the air with shock when a car sounded its

horn. It wasn't just the fumes from these vehicles that sullied the air. It was their dreadful noises as well.

One of the questions that played in Maynard's mind like an irritating tune was, "Why me?" And the only answer he'd been given was, "Because you're a result of something you do back there." There'd been no explanation of that incomprehensible answer. And there would never be one. In the next few hours or days or however long it took to alter the history of human cloning, something that would affect his entire life also had to happen. And it had to happen naturally. If he attempted to force it, if he tried too hard, everything might change. Everything. So, while nature took its course, Maynard had to concentrate on saving humankind. For a seventeen-year-old boy, that was quite enough. For a seventeen-year-old boy, that was far too much. The pressure made him feel crucial and inadequate at the same time. Like a king gazing up at a huge sky full of stars, he felt important yet insignificant.

There was also a more mundane reason he'd been chosen. He was not ill with botulism. The scientists had never developed a resistance gene for the botulism toxin so no one could buy immunity for their children. Maynard was lucky that he had not yet succumbed to *Clostridium botulinum*. Mercifully, he had been spared the awful vomiting, continuous diarrhoea, the breathing difficulties, distorted vision and paralysis – and the death – that the mutes had inflicted on the world.

Maynard had a bird's unerring sense of direction. It was dusk when he reached Patrick Finch's house. The garage door had been daubed with KILL THE BABY FARMER –

obviously a reaction to the press conference. One down-stairs window of the Finches' fortress was boarded up. Looking around to make sure that no one was watching, Maynard slipped into the entry at the side of the house and crept towards the bush where he guessed that he'd lost his watch. He got down on his hands and knees and foraged under the hedge with his fingers and, at the same time, he peered into the vicious bushes. Often, he stopped scaveng-ing underneath so he could use both hands to part the hedge carefully and, thankful for his night vision, explore the tangle of twigs. Any one of the thorns, snags or forks could have hooked the watch from his wrist, but he saw nothing. Among the decaying leaves below the bushes, he found only litter. An empty cigarette box, two discarded crisp packets, a grimy wrapping from a chocolate bar and a receipt for a mobile phone could tell him a lot about this community's preoccupations but it did not unearth his watch. He closed his eyes and muttered a quiet curse. For the moment, all he could do was hope that it hadn't fallen into the wrong hands.

Returning to the front of the property, he checked that his hood was pulled well down over his forehead. He didn't want to make it easy for the security cameras that he assumed would be trained on the path to the front door. He extracted the envelope from his pocket, ready to deliver the letter that Patrick Finch would dismiss as hate mail.

4

Jordan Finch was mystified. In his bedroom, he'd removed the back of the watch and he found himself staring at a mechanism that was like no other he'd seen. He felt like a pathologist who had just cut into a dead body and found the electronics of a sophisticated robot rather than the bloody organs of a human being. The technology was totally new to him. Even more surprising, there was no trace of a battery – not a conventional, recognizable one anyway. Jordan replaced the back plate, turned the watch over and scrutinized the face once more. There was definitely no solar panel as an energy source. But the watch was undoubtedly working, so what was fuelling it? What was the power source? He didn't have a clue.

He slipped the watch on to his left wrist. When he tapped its side, the time and date disappeared. Instead, the screen split into three boxes. The first read, *Pulse 78*. The second, *Temp 37.2*, was clearly his body temperature. The third section of the screen worried him. It was showing, *Met Con: 1*. What did that mean? Anyway, when he slipped a piece of paper between his wrist and the watch, the display went blank. That proved he was right that there was a sensor on its base plate. Jordan took the watch off again. He decided to poke around inside it a bit more.

His mobile phone rang with the shrill tone of a desperately hungry young bird. It was Tim. "Hi. Club tonight? Eight o'clock?"

"No, I can't," Jordan moaned. "I've been grounded. You know, after last night's party – even though I saved Mum and Dad when I got back. I disarmed a mad petrol bomber – heroically."

"Really?"

"Yeah. As sure as one of your dad's promises just before an election."

"Complete fantasy, then." Tim paused and then added, "I'll come round to you. OK? I'll bring Neat."

"Anita?"

"Yeah. We're getting it together."

"Since when?" Jordan asked.

"Since a few hours ago."

"No. Are you kidding?"

"Neat's OK." Tim's giant smile almost transmitted itself through the telephone network.

"Yeah, but. . ." Jordan hesitated. "Are you sure it's Neat?"

The twins were almost impossible to tell apart and it had been known for them to do a swap. If they had to take a maths test at different times, Anita would sit in for Myleene because she was terrible with numbers. If it was art or English, Myleene would return the favour. They swapped lessons as freely as they swapped lipsticks. They also swapped detentions as frequently as they swapped dresses. The sisters had even confessed to Jordan that, when one of them wanted to ditch a boyfriend, the other sometimes turned up to do the dumping. They reckoned it avoided a lot of unpleasantness and heartache that way. They usually got away with it because physically they were identical. The two girls were slightly different, though. Neat spoke faster, more nervously, and she always smelled minty because she was addicted to extra-strong mints. Their exam-switching stunt backfired when the school got suspicious because a clearly hopeless Myleene kept turning in brilliant maths marks. Now, the school always made sure that, whenever possible, they took their exams and detentions at the same time.

Tim said, "I gave her a maths problem and a packet of Polos. It's Neat all right."

Putting the phone down, Jordan found himself standing between the full-length mirror on his bedroom door and the smaller one attached to his wardrobe. For a while, he watched copies of himself stretching into the distance. He swayed one way and the other, watching the virtual Jordans mimic him uncannily. He felt as if he were at the head of a nightmarish queue at a bus stop, suddenly realizing that no buses were ever going to arrive but more and more doubles were going to line up and mock him. A faint noise in the hall provided the excuse to dash downstairs, away from the hypnotic and unsettling series of images. On the mat by the front door there was a letter, addressed to Patrick Finch in red ink. "Dad!" Jordan shouted. "Post's come."

"At this time of night? Don't open it!"

Jordan weighed the envelope in his hand. It was far too light to contain anything explosive and, he noticed, the flap had not been sealed down. Walking into the living room, he said, "Too late. It's already open. No dodgy powders or anything. Just red ink. It's going to tell you your work's not everybody's cup of herbal tea."

Patrick waved his hand. "Another militant bunny-hugger or bible-basher. Put it straight in the bin, Jordan."

"And miss a literary masterpiece? No chance. What's the betting it's in capitals?" He pulled out the piece of notepaper and unfolded it. "Oh. A quiet protest. Surprise, surprise. It's not even abuse. It's making a point. Listen. *The name of the first person to do anything is for ever linked with the teething problems. It's better to wait and be known as the scientist who got it right.* High-class hate mail, wouldn't you say?"

"Bin," Patrick repeated.

The window was still boarded up because the emergency glazier had not yet turned up to put right what a protester had shattered earlier. The workman wasn't late because he couldn't find the Finches' house. He'd made innumerable visits before because the Finches were regular clients. Patrick and Gwen had cleared away the glittery mess but, when Jordan's mum got wearily to her feet and walked to the computer, she trod carefully in case any pieces of glass still lurked in the carpet. She marked the video record so the police could capture the latest caller's image for their database. Gwen also needed to check that whoever had delivered the letter had walked back down the garden path and away without leaving any nasty surprises. She didn't really believe that such a polite protest message would come with any sort of device but she had to be sure. The bricks, burning rags and firebombs usually arrived with a torrent of four-letter words but the police warned the family at every opportunity that they had to be on their guard against fresh tactics.

Looking up from the screen, Gwen remarked, "Looks like the one who turned up in the garden last night. Young, possibly quite handsome – it's hard to say with a hood over his eyes – but probably a good physique under those clothes. What do you think, Jordan?"

Jordan took a quick look at a replay of the hooded figure coming up the path. "Not my type." Realizing immediately that his mum wasn't in the mood for joking, he studied a still for a few seconds and then said, "Could well be him. But. . ." He shrugged. "Can't be sure." He peered inside the envelope to check again that it was empty, then screwed it up and threw it in the bin. He tapped the letter and said to his dad, "PP's got a good point, though, hasn't he?"

"PP?"

"The Polite Protester."

Jordan's dad was not in a state of mind to listen to another anonymous person with yet more advice. His front window was in pieces and his best suit was at the cleaners, having the mess removed. On top of that, he was on edge, waiting for important experimental results. "We're going to get it right first time. OK? I don't need aggro from my own family. Not now. It's a crucial few weeks for me. The research we're doing will shape the future of the human race." He drank the limeflower tea that would calm his busy mind, reduce his stress levels and soothe him to sleep tonight.

Kept indoors by his parents for his latest misdemeanour, Jordan wasn't in the best of moods either. "How does it feel to be God?"

"That's rubbish, Jordan. How often do I have to. . ." He sighed with exasperation.

"There's a better time for this, Jordan," his mother put in.

"Yeah, but. . ." Jordan threw himself down into a chair and looked at his dad. "You're a doctor. You cure things. That's it. Nothing in the job description about reinventing human beings."

Patrick replied, "At your age, babies aren't on your mind – I'm glad to say. But you don't understand how desperate couples get for a child who'll carry their own genes. It's a biological urge, an incredibly powerful instinct, and it's seen humans through thousands of years."

"I can see myself with kids one day. It's supposed to be what life's all about." Jordan had never had qualms about discussing sex. Living with a man who specialized in fertility, Jordan had had a surfeit of sex education. He knew every single nut and bolt. He also knew about dedication to a cause – his dad specialized in that too – but Jordan knew a lot less about love. His dad's first love had always been his work, not his family. "I'll tell you what I do understand: the attraction between boys and girls, sex, a fifty-fifty mix of two people. It's about babies coming in families, not shops. The future's not a test-tube factory, is it?"

"You bet it is. There's too many things to go wrong in the lottery of sex. The future lies in proper design." A difficult day had taken a big bite out of Patrick's patience so he didn't launch into his usual lecture on the benefits of leaving nothing to chance and removing faulty genes. He didn't go on about clones being perfect reproductions – perfectly healthy reproductions. He confined himself to one sound-bite. "We need to be the architects of our own future, our own evolution."

Jordan let out a grunt. "Sounds like playing God to me."

"Are you so sure God's down on cloning? If you take the Bible literally, the first two human clones were Adam and Eve. To a lot of people, the prospect of having a genetically perfect baby in their own image is the bee's knees. If it was good enough for God when he made Adam and Eve, it's good enough for my clients."

"Ah, well, it's no big deal then. You're not going to be the first because God beat you to it, so what's the rush?"

"I'm beginning to wish we hadn't grounded you."

Two blocks away, Maynard sat in a quiet alleyway, earpiece in place, listening to the Finches' entire conversation. The reception was a bit crackly but his bugs were working beautifully.

Maynard was glad he'd brought some eavesdropping gadgets. They were the size of particles of dust and right now they were floating around Patrick Finch's home with the rest of the household dust. Jordan Finch had taken out the letter that Maynard had peppered with the light-powered specks. Eventually they would settle, at least one bug in every room of the house. It was old technology, but effective. From now on, Maynard would be able to listen in on Patrick Finch chatting with his family and visitors. With any luck, Maynard would hear all of the biologist's telephone conversations as well.

Already Patrick had confirmed that Maynard had arrived at exactly the right time. It was those vital cloning experiments that Maynard needed to influence. Maynard had also learned that there was antagonism between Patrick and his son. The rift between them was something that Maynard might be able to exploit.

Even so, Maynard was fascinated by the notion of a family. He envied the security and homeliness of it all. Even if there were disagreements, there was also care and support. Maynard didn't have a mother and, to prevent psychological damage, he'd been separated from his father as soon as he was able to go to school. Maynard was good at independence, bad at relationships. Yes, he was intrigued by family.

Downstairs, the clatter was the sound of the glazier removing the wooden board and the remains of the old window. This time, he was going to use an incredibly expensive, toughened, almost unbreakable type of glass. "They'll need one of those special missiles to get through this," he said with undue confidence. He was not used to the superhuman fury that the opponents of cloning could summon. They went thermonuclear regularly.

The police, as useless as ever, had reported that the youth discovered in the Finches' garden was not in their electronic identity parade. He was now, of course, but he was an anonymous entry. And he scored a 77 per cent likeness with tonight's wildcat postman. It would have been a better match but the cameras had not captured enough of his facial features. And there was a visible mark, possibly a scratch, on his face this time that wasn't there before. Even so, as Gwen Finch suspected, he was almost certainly the same person. He was definitely wearing the same clothes.

Upstairs, Jordan sniffed for mint and listened closely to make sure it was Anita. "You're like two peas in a pod, you and Myleene," he said. "Exactly the same genes. Must be weird."

"Not to us. We've never known anything else but, yes, it feels like we're two halves of the same person. We were wrapping our arms round each other before we were even born. When she feels sad, I feel sad as well. We'll never split up."

Jordan asked, "But how would you feel if something happened to Myleene?"

"Like what?"

"I don't want to be too morbid but . . . I really mean, what would your mum and dad think if she went off to . . . I don't know . . . Australia, and got eaten by a shark or something?"

"That's horrid."

"Yes, but I don't mean it. It's just theoretical. How would they feel about it, though? 'Well, we've lost a daughter but we haven't lost that set of genes because we've still got Neat.'"

"That's the trouble with you, Jordan. You're so . . . matter of fact. A person's . . . a person – flesh and blood, not nuts and bolts. Of course they wouldn't. Only you'd think like that. They'd be shattered."

"I'd be happy to feed my sister to a shark," Tim put in. "Though I'm not sure any self-respecting shark would. . ."

A look from Anita shut them both up.

In the semi-darkness, the long wall seemed to stretch to infinity. It was topped with a bundle of razor wire and every fifty metres there was a pole supporting a video camera. Unlike human guards, these electronic lookouts were always vigilant. They never got tired, bored or sidetracked. They never stopped looking. On one side of the brick wall was the British headquarters of the Finch Private Fertility Clinic, securely wrapped up. On the other side was SPACE City, the protesters' vulnerable and ragged camp. In between was a mass of graffiti.

The inhabitants of the Save People and Animals from Cloning Experiments camp were like mutes. Several were clustered around the main gates with their placards. Some others were cooking vegetables over an open fire. A few had gathered round a guitarist and were singing softly. Two others were erecting more tents. Within Westford, SPACE City was still spreading, encroaching on a field that led to a wood.

Inside the prison walls, a construction company was erecting some new outbuildings and adding two further storeys to the main block of the clinic. Clearly Patrick Finch was not short of wealthy donors. The Finch Private Fertility Clinic was growing faster than the protesters' camp.

"Hi."

Surprised by the tentative greeting, Maynard replied, "Er, hello."

"Looks like you're dressed warm," the young woman remarked. She had a soft voice and, in talking to a stranger, seemed to be fighting a natural shyness. "Are you here to join us?"

Maynard had decided to infiltrate the activists. "Yes."

The girl smiled. "I'm Gaia Queen."

"Really?"

Her smile widened, but she wasn't poking fun at Maynard when she replied, "No. We don't use real names here – in case the police are listening in. In case they've got a mole in here somehow."

"A mole?"

"A spy."

"Ah."

"If you're genuine, we can sort out some accommodation and food for you. It's not exactly five star."

Maynard nodded towards the grim wall. "The clinic's well protected. Has anyone ever got inside?"

Four activists in balaclavas were moving along the perimeter, throwing stones up at each hated camera in turn until they heard the satisfying sound of breakage.

"Not without getting arrested straight away," Gaia Queen answered. "One way or another, we get two arrested most days. As soon as they're bailed, they're back here. On duty."

Both of them looked towards the main gate as a lorry left for the night.

"Have you ever tried to smuggle anyone in on a builders' truck?"

"Quite a few times. They're too good at searching everything that goes on site, though. They get found and taken away by the police. And before you ask," she added, "our people have made lots of applications for jobs with the builders. We got a couple taken on but the clinic's contract says the builders are only allowed to use workers who've been with them for five years or more. That knocks out our recruits. Finch and his security people have thought of everything."

Maynard's long sigh sounded like a sudden chill wind. Without his watch, getting on the other side of the wall was going to be very difficult. Perhaps impossible. He was going to have to be very creative to penetrate the clinic and immediately his mind turned to Jordan Finch, the argumentative son.

Keen to prolong the conversation with easily the most fanciable boy in the encampment, Gaia Queen said, "The police think we're extremists but the real extremists are in there." She jerked her head towards the wall. "If only we could get at them. I'd shoot all vivisectionists, I would, totally."

It was odd to hear a heartfelt threat from such a sweet and gentle voice. Maynard looked into her face. Her smile had a chilling innocence. He had no doubt that she was seething inside. He asked, "What exactly do you object to?"

"Using animals in research."

"Not humans?"

"Humans have a choice," Gaia Queen replied. "What about you?"

Maynard thought about it for a moment. "I'm here for the clones that are born defective. They don't have a choice either. Human or animal."

Believing that she had detected something sincere, strong and single-minded – yet also sad and strange – about this striking newcomer, Gaia Queen nodded. The stubble growing on his chin and the scratches and shadows falling across his handsome face added an appealing layer of mystery. "Good to have you on board. You need a name."

"I'm. . ."

She put up her hand. "Don't tell me. The police, remember. You can be Space Cadet. Yes. Why not? Space Cadet."

The doorway was small and opaque but still it reminded Maynard of the one that he had formed to bring him to this place. He pushed aside the flimsy nylon and crawled into the tent. No, it wasn't luxury but it was big enough to sleep in, it was dry and it kept out most of the wind. He lay down on his back, the groundsheet offering little relief from the ridges of hard earth below, and felt the sides closing him in. The blue skin, made black by the night, swayed gently in the breeze as if it were breathing. Of course, Maynard had never been inside a real womb but the tent brought to mind his first nine months of life – sort-of life – growing inside an artificial one.

At least he could leave the tent at any time. Without his watch, other gateways were all closed to him. Maynard felt claustrophobic, trapped in the pre-cloning world, a living exhibit in a museum.

He fitted the earpiece into his ear, closed his eyes, and let the ghostly conversations from the Finch family drift through him. It was like listening to three radio stations at the same time. Patrick was talking to someone, almost certainly his wife. Elsewhere in the house Jordan chatted with a boy and at least one girl. In the background, music was playing. Without recording and editing equipment, Maynard found it difficult to filter one exchange from the other. As far as he could gather, Jordan was comparing clones with natural twins while Patrick and Gwen Finch were chatting about falling sperm counts.

Maynard's eyes opened in the dark and he muttered, "Yes. Of course!"

He woke when the sun turned the nylon skin into a light blue. He unzipped the flap of the tent and looked out, still surprised that there was no snow. Amazingly, there were clusters of faded daffodils and two early birds were playing tugs-of-war with obstinate worms. Beyond the starlings was the ugly wall of the fertility clinic. In Maynard's time, there was no such barricade. Cloning had become accepted and it did not need protection from protesters. More than that, human cloning was celebrated. For many men, it was the only way to pass on their genes to the next generation. In Maynard's time, there were no daffodils or starlings either. A lot of plants refused to grow and many birds had flown away to warmer climates.

The mood in the encampment was sky high. Over

breakfast, Gaia Queen was almost jumping up and down with excitement. The tabloids were teeming with pictures from the press conference, especially snaps of Finch's startled face at the moment of impact. The caption writers had had a field day. *Finch is sitting duck. Finch makes feathers fly. The yolk's on him*. None of it brought Maynard's task a millimetre closer to completion but the activists' laughter was infectious anyway. The bedraggled group needed meaningless little triumphs to keep its spirits up, to keep alive the possibility of major triumphs later.

Surrounded by Gaia Queen, Tadpole and Anti Clone, Maynard felt as if he was undergoing some sort of initiation test. "Gaia here says you want to get inside," said Tadpole.

Maynard nodded. "Yes."

Anti Clone asked, "One: how do you get in? Two: what do you do when you're in there?"

"Well, I've got an idea."

"Like?"

"I know Finch's son, Jordan."

Tadpole interrupted. "We've all shouted at him across the street. We all know him like that. Do you *really* know him?"

Astounded, Maynard watched Tadpole pull a cigarette from a box and light it. Trying to stay focused, he responded, "Er. . . We got quite close, actually."

"And?"

"You shouldn't shout at him," Maynard replied. "He's on your side . . . *our* side."

"Interesting," Gaia Queen murmured thoughtfully.

Anti Clone ignored her. "So what if he is your mate?

How does that get you into his dad's clinic and, even if you did get in," she said, clearly not believing that Maynard could ever penetrate the site, "what would you do?"

"Anti Clone's been arrested more than anyone else in SPACE," Gaia Queen explained. "She's tried every which way to get in, totally."

Space Cadet nodded. Now he understood Anti Clone's aggression. She was scared that a mere newcomer might succeed straight away where she had already failed many times. Her pride was just as strong as her dedication to the cause. "It's a simple idea," Maynard said. "I persuade him we both need treatment at the clinic, a sperm test or at least a check-up. Then I go in with him."

"Huh. I offered to be an egg donor," Anti Clone replied, "but it didn't work. I didn't get past the vetting. Real name, false name, it didn't make any difference. They knew straight away I was an activist."

"They can vet me all they like," Space Cadet said. "They won't trace anything. Not a thing on me." As he walked away, he added over his shoulder, "I'll go and get on with it." That way he avoided Anti Clone's awkward second question. What would he do when he got inside his own birthplace? He knew what he should do but he was beginning to doubt his instructions.

Not even the most thoroughly dusted and vacuumed house could be purged of every tiny bug. Usually the surveillance dust lasted for days, even weeks, before the specks malfunctioned, got swept away or drifted into dark corners where light could not power them any more. Signals from the Finches' house were still quite strong. After eavesdropping on Jordan's conversations, it was easy for Maynard to decide how to bump into him.

Maynard had overheard Jordan arranging to meet Tim "and the others" at KFC. Once Gaia Queen had educated her cadet on the vital subject of Kentucky Fried Chicken, he decided to gatecrash the group at the restaurant. First, Gaia Queen disguised the scratches on his cheeks and hands with make-up and supervised the buying of less conspicuous clothes for him.

On the way to the shopping arcade, Maynard could hardly miss the giant figure gazing longingly through the window of an electrical store. He stopped beside Lights Out, looked around and said, "Where's. . .?" Not knowing what to call Lights Out's short companion, Maynard drew a finger across his own forehead and said, "Manchester United." Then he put out a flat hand, palm down, on a level with his own chest, indicating the homeless man's height.

Lights Out understood at once. "Gone." Abandoned and downcast, he looked as out of place as Maynard. At least he was clean. Overnight, he'd had a shower and laundered his clothes at the homeless shelter.

To Maynard, Lights Out also looked lean and hungry. Maynard hesitated for a second and then said, "I'm going to get a meal. Do you want a Kentucky Fried Chicken?" As soon as he said it, Maynard cursed himself. Lights Out would cramp his style in the encounter with Jordan Finch and make the biologist's son suspicious. But for years Maynard had been brainwashed into turning his back on mutes and ignoring their obvious need. For him, that was normal, virtually automatic. Now, in this old world that was new to Maynard, it was time to change, to turn his back on his training and his primitive impulse. This was a time of humanity and vitality.

Lights Out was eager but puzzled at the invitation. "You have pounds?"

"Money, yes."

Lights Out licked his lips and turned on a childish smile as easily as switching on a light.

"Come on. This way, I think." Even if Gaia Queen had not told Maynard where the fast food shop was, his heightened sense of smell would have guided him unerringly to it.

Lights Out nodded hungrily. He knew where the restaurant was, although he was more used to scavenging among the scraps at its rear and in the bins along the street. He'd smelled the KFC shop often enough but he'd never been in it. He had never seen a complete meal.

As they walked, Lights Out gazed at Maynard from the collar of his smart waterproof jacket down to his shoes. Perplexed, Lights Out said, "Good . . . *adeshda*."

Seeing Lights Out's envious glances, Maynard guessed what he meant. "Clothes?"

"*Da*. Yes."

Maynard did not have to explain his sudden change because the sight and smell of the restaurant distracted Lights Out. He strode out and Maynard had to quicken his step to keep up.

Maynard had seen Jordan Finch just once in the dark

but, equipped with a cat's genes for night vision, it was enough. Recognizing Jordan in the restaurant was easy. Apart from two families with toddlers, Jordan and his friends were the only other group in the place. They were the ones creating all of the noise, laughter mainly. Maynard kept an eye on them and listened. He did not have to be particularly discreet because they were too wrapped up in themselves to notice another boy watching them.

By the time Maynard looked back at Lights Out, his carton contained little but stripped bones.

From Jordan's group, a girl called Myleene sauntered towards the counter to buy more drinks. As she passed, she looked at Lights Out. Then, when she joined the queue, she glanced at him again and smiled. Quick to spot an opportunity, Maynard jumped up. "I'll get you another meal," he said to Lights Out and joined the queue behind Myleene. Leaning forward, he said to the girl, "My friend wanted to say hello to you but he's a bit shy."

Myleene gazed over Maynard's shoulder. "So he sent you?"

"Well, his English isn't so good but he needs another bag of chips."

"Looks like he needs more than chips. Get him a family bucket," she suggested, not entirely seriously.

Maynard was amazed that they sold meals designed for a family. He was used only to meals for one.

Interested, Myleene asked, "Where did you meet?"

Maynard tried to interpret the tone of her bold question and failed. It was halfway between astonishment and admiration. "He's a mu. . . He's homeless."

"Is that right?" she said. "I'd never have guessed."

If it was admiration, Maynard could not tell if Myleene admired him for helping the homeless or if she admired Lights Out for being physically outstanding. Of course, Maynard couldn't understand anyone being impressed by such an outlandish shape. Lights Out was far from the accepted norm of attractiveness.

From his table, Lights Out looked up at Myleene in much the same way that earlier he'd eyed a bag of chips, a box of chicken and the window display of electrical goods. He smiled broadly.

Myleene returned a slight nod of acknowledgement. Tired of flirting by proxy, she asked, "Look, er, why don't you come over? You and your friend. Then he can say hello."

"Well, we'd love to . . . but, no, better not," Maynard replied, playing hard to get. "We don't want to . . . you know." He inclined his head towards Lights Out.

"No problem," Myleene said. "It's not easy to embarrass us. Tim over there's got an MP for a dad. We still talk to him. And my mum's in the police."

Maynard hesitated just long enough before he agreed. "OK. Thanks."

Between mouthfuls, Lights Out explained in stilted language how he came to be in Westford. "I saw . . . shopping list." He shrugged, signifying that he knew he hadn't used the right words but that he couldn't get any closer. "Telephon there." His grease-stained fingers went momentarily to the side of his face, holding an imaginary phone. "No . . . line."

"A mobile," said Myleene, pulling hers out of a pocket and holding it up for him to see.

"*Da*. And sandwich toaster." His eyes lit up and this time there was no hesitation. He had learned the magical words as if they were the password that would allow him into heaven. "Then I know I have to come to England."

"You came all the way from deepest Russia because you saw a sandwich toaster in a catalogue?" Tim spluttered, almost spilling his Pepsi.

"*Da*. Yes. *Ochyen karosho*. Great good."

They weren't laughing at Lights Out. They were laughing at the notion. It also struck them as funny that, of all of the things a homeless man might crave, Lights Out had put a sandwich toaster at the top of his list. It was a luxury that couldn't possibly be of any use to him.

Myleene added, "Why not? Any place that's got sandwich toasters must be doing all right."

Lights Out looked from Myleene to Anita in wonder – as if he'd seen an offer of two sandwich toasters for the price of one. "Yes, good."

None of the group of friends had ever had to rough it so they regarded Lights Out as an exotic curiosity. Only people who had never experienced his way of life could possibly view it as romantic. Even though Jordan had been trained to be suspicious of strangers, he saw no reason to be wary of Lights Out. He was utterly harmless. Tim, perhaps intimidated by Lights Out's physical size, put an arm possessively round Anita's shoulders.

Myleene merely smiled at Tim's unsubtle body language. Having much the same taste in boys as her twin, shunning the conventionally handsome like Maynard in favour of the big and cute, Myleene knew that Neat would be drooling over Lights Out. The difference between them was that Myleene looked available.

"Where are you living?"

"What?" He pointed to both of his ears and shrugged helplessly.

"I think he's a bit deaf," Maynard explained.

"Maybe sound has trouble penetrating the thin air at his altitude," Jordan suggested.

"Where do you live?" Myleene shouted.

Lights Out waved a hand loosely. "Around."

"How about you?" Jordan asked Maynard.

"The other side of town."

Immediately, Jordan's brow creased. Suddenly alert, he said, "The other side from what?"

It was a mistake. As soon as he'd said it, Maynard regretted it. The KFC was in the city centre, so the other side of town didn't make sense. He couldn't say that he lived on the opposite side to the Finches' house because he couldn't admit that he knew where Jordan lived. And he couldn't yet admit that he was living in SPACE City. Maynard did his best to squirm out of the corner. "Erm . . . Sorry. Your school. I overheard you saying something about it earlier."

"Cool it, Jordan," Myleene said. "Less of the secret agent stuff. Please." Turning to Maynard, she asked, "Are you taking Lights Out home with you?"

"Well. . ." Maynard saw Lights Out's imploring expression and knew that he had no choice. "Yes. Sure." He also

55

saw the twins' faint smiles. They were both thinking that it would be easier to meet Lights Out again if he had a proper place to stay. As if a tent outside the Finch Private Fertility Clinic were a proper place to stay.

6

Zadie was twenty-two. She was at the peak of her reproductive powers. But for a mute, though, fertility never scaled the heights. She lay on the cold hard platform as a male tried his luck. Three other men watched and waited. And Zadie dreamed of a child.

Entombed under Westford's Highpoint Fertility Clinic, the air was blue with fumes from the fire and it stung her eyes. It carried the smell of meat, though. Zadie twisted her head to see, further along the underground platform, mutes cooking the morning's haul of rats and squirrels. Beyond them, another man and woman were attempting to breed. A small curious audience stood nearby and encouraged them, but not with any great confidence. The chances of a working sperm meeting a viable egg were slender at best. At least it was warm underground. Not warm enough to remove any clothes, though, and that made the sex appear even more shabby.

In a lot of countries, heatwaves and droughts were killing people with abandon. Paradoxically, people were freezing to death in Britain. Because global warming had disrupted the Gulf Stream, Britain and northern Europe no longer simmered in warm water from the tropics. The temperature plummeted and a mini ice age beckoned.

While Zadie's mate issued exasperated grunts, she

thought of babies, food and the climate. She did not hold him. She didn't want to touch him any more than necessary. Her right hand cushioned her head against the concrete platform and her other arm stretched out limply like a doll's. As always, she was tired. Her weak heart had never pumped enough blood through her body. She had an intense pain in the centre of her chest, as if it were gripped by a vice, and the spasms spread relentlessly into her throbbing left arm and lower jaw.

Her enlarged tongue lay heavily in her mouth like an unwanted slab of meat. Over the years it had become totally numb. The nerves had been destroyed because she had bitten into it countless times. To her teeth, it was an unavoidable object. At least the accidental bites weren't painful any longer but she could take no pleasure in eating. No feeling remained through the rough scar tissue. Every small piece of food that she pushed carefully into the narrow cavity above her lifeless tongue tasted like squirrel.

She could take no pleasure in sex, either. It varied between painful and unfeeling. But this passionless act was a duty to be done. Over and over again. Mutes had lost so much of their health over the years but, cruelly, not their desire to reproduce. They saw themselves as a separate, persecuted and dwindling race. They could not let that race die out, no matter how much hardship they suffered.

None of Zadie's lovers had ever kissed her because of that tongue. Because she couldn't swallow properly, food lodged in her mouth and throat, rotted and made her breath foul. Even so, she was not short of lovers. There was always a queue. Sometimes she was so sore and dirty that it felt as if she'd tried to breed with every male mute in Westford. Maybe she had. Some of them she'd tried lots of times. Her weak eyesight was a godsend. Most of them were ugly and disgusting but, as her partner stood up, adjusted his trousers and went to get a barbecued rat as his reward, Zadie told herself that beggars can't be choosers.

7

Patrick no longer jumped in surprise when a stone hit some part of his car on the way into the clinic. He was incapable of being startled. He was angry, though. His windscreen was now decorated with three tiny stars where the glass had started to fracture. The car body held some sort of perverse record for the number of repairs and re-sprays. He was well on the way to establishing another record for the number of windscreen replacements. All because of those damned terrorists. With disdain, Patrick drove rapidly past the ones who had chained themselves to the large entrance gate. Security men with huge wire cutters were detaching them one-by-one and releasing them like hooked fish back into a pond. Of course, they'd volunteer to get hooked again overnight.

Today, Patrick ignored the ginseng tonic on his desk and charged straight to the animal house. He didn't mind the experiments on mice, rabbits, cats and dogs. The fate of farm animals – sheep, cattle, pigs and goats – didn't bother him either. After all, thousands of them were killed every day for food. But primates were different. Seeing the laboratory monkeys always sent an unpleasant shiver down his spine. Patrick could not look at the hands of a chimpanzee wrapped around the bars of its cage without thinking of a human being. If the animal's hands had not been so leathery, they could almost belong to a person. And chimps and people had 99 per cent of their DNA in common. In the mortuary, Patrick tried not to think of that kinship while he watched the post-mortem examination of the latest sub-standard clone.

"He's a big fellah," Kayleigh said as she bundled the dead chimpanzee over on to his back. He was slightly curled up, like a foetus. "Too big for his age and he's got the usual swollen tongue." For the sake of the recording, she said, "OK. He's in dorsal recumbency. Rigor mortis has set in, so stand by for some effort and unpleasantness." To perform the examination, Kayleigh needed the chimpanzee's fore and hind limbs well apart, displaying the chest and abdomen. "Here we go." She heaved energetically on each limb in turn to stretch it out. There was a dreadful crunching sound as she pushed each leg down. "Never got used to how stiff they get after a few hours," she remarked. "It's hard work. Not like humans." She touched a button on the table so the overhead digital camera took the first picture. "He's definitely too big but there's no external injuries or flaws." Then she plunged the scalpel into the mid-line of the abdomen and slit the animal open to expose a glistening white seam of tendon from its breastbone to its genitals. "I'm going to incise the linea alba and take a look at the contents of the guts." The technician took a deep breath and said, "My least favourite bit." As she sliced into it, an overpowering smell like no other filled the room. Patrick wasn't ready for the appalling stench and he had to swallow to keep the contents of his own stomach in place. Kayleigh glanced at her boss and said, "The extraction fan's on. It won't last too long."

She extended the cut along the line of the chimp's last rib, mopping up the yellowy perineal fluid as she went, completely revealing the muddle of internal organs. She took another photograph. "First the liver," Kayleigh said. "Mmm. Should be reddish brown but it's orange and bloated. Not as firm to the touch as it should be either. Strangely rough." Carefully, she scooped it out in both gloved hands and placed it on the balance. "Yeah. Twice the weight it should be. It's got to go to the pathologist." She cut through a piece of the misshapen liver with her scalpel and pressed the fresh surface on to a glass slide so she could examine the smear for abnormal cells under a microscope afterwards. "What else? The spleen's a healthy brown-red, nice and firm. No problem." Kayleigh pulled back the lace-like curtain of fatty tissue that covered most of the animal's intestines and stomach. "I wish fingers weren't the best tool in this business but they are. Let's feel our way through the digestive system." With a wince on her face, her fingers started at the stomach and followed the soft string of small intestines and then the large intestines down to the anal canal. "Blocked," she pronounced. "Ugh, nasty." She stood upright for a moment, sucked in air, and then bent down to the exposed innards again. Poised over the gut, she said, "Time for a clothes peg on the nose again." The second stench hit them as she delved inside. "Phew. Nothing here but its last meal. Thank God." She moved aside the tortuous tangle of intestines to display the major blood vessels, the kidneys, urinary tract and bladder. Then she took another photo. "I'll dissect the kidneys later but I can't see or feel any obvious problems." She took a few tissue samples and swabs and then wiped down her latex gloves.

"Right. Time to work our way up, starting with the diaphragm." The sheet of muscle that separated the abdomen and thorax was tinged white and healthy. She carved into the skin along the centre of the chest, all the way to the neck. The ribcage flapped open under Kayleigh's expert hands. She picked up a gruesome pair of strong scissors and began to cut into the ribcage. "Not too difficult in a young animal," she told Patrick. "The bigger ones need a hacksaw."

Even so, Patrick cringed at the grotesque sound of cracking ribs. Trying to make light of it, he said, "Steady. I've just had breakfast."

"Spare ribs?" Kayleigh asked with a smile.

"Thankfully not."

She put down the scissors, pushed back the chimp's ribs to get a good look at the thoracic cavity, and took a sample of the fluid inside. "No haemorrhaging, infections or tumours on the walls of the thorax," she reported, taking more photographs. "The lungs are underdeveloped but not far short of normal. Light and spongy, typical red in colour." Squashed between her fingers, the lung tissue felt like a bath sponge and crackled slightly. "No other abnormalities really. The purple patches are just where the tissue's rubbed against the ribcage. I'm going to do a pluck later."

"A pluck?" Patrick queried.

"Yes. I'm going to lift out the lungs, heart, trachea and larynx in one for weighing and further examination. For now, though, come and take a closer look at this."

"What?"

"The heart. It's really bloated. I mean gross." She pulled down the camera for some close-ups. "It's in the right place for a heart but . . . I hardly recognize it. The pericardium's fit to burst. The muscles are flabby and I bet the chamber walls are too thick. I'll dissect it later to confirm that. Anyway, the heart's your top problem, not helped by a dicky liver and blocked intestine."

Patrick shook his head and swore under his breath. Here he was, trying desperately to improve the lot of infertile human beings, to find a detour around nature's mistakes, and nature was not co-operating. Was nature that callous and spiteful towards humans? It looked as if the cloning process itself was damaging the genes involved in growth. A gene called IGF2R normally slowed growth when body parts reached the right size but during cloning, their gene seemed to be switched off so the animal's organs swelled until they were useless. Goddamn it! He was trying to do the world a favour and yet nature was conspiring against him.

Kayleigh was working directly above the heart, cutting through the hoops of cartilage that formed the windpipe, making more repulsive crunching noises. "Nothing worth noting here. I suppose you want me to see how fertile he was going to be, though."

"Yes. And go into the brain, will you? Is that overgrown as well? Then put all your findings on computer. I'll need to study everything later."

As Patrick left, Kayleigh had a scalpel in one hand and a small testicle in the other.

Outside, Patrick emptied his lungs of the foul air and drew in a deep breath. Now he needed the tonic that his secretary provided instead of coffee. It would settle the contents of his stomach and wash the taste of putrescence from his mouth.

Patrick Finch was an enigma, full of contradictions. He was a doctor but he mistrusted medicine. He consumed fresh fruit and fibre for his digestive tract, fennel tea for flatulence, fish for his heart, extract of saw palmetto berries for his prostate, cranberry juice for his urinary tract, organic potatoes and pasta for energy. At home, the Finches' larder smelled like a health food shop. He avoided alcohol, coffee, dairy products, fatty meat, drugs and, of course, doctors. He cared so much for children and childless couples that he would trample over any obstacle to be the first to free people from the cruellest of nature's jokes: infertility. In public, he appeared brash and certain of the value of cloning but privately he suffered guilt and doubts that he had not even admitted to his family. Embarking on a course of action that would decide the destiny of the human species made Patrick more powerful than prime ministers and presidents, and deadlier than disease. Standing at a turning point in human history blurred the lines that divided the ethical from the unethical, the safe from the dangerous.

The tonic helped Patrick but the grim taste of decay lingered in his nose and mouth.

When he turned on his computer, it directed him immediately to his message board. He had been exchanging heated messages for days with someone calling himself

Churchman. Patrick assumed that Churchman was a nickname rather than a surname. He also assumed that Churchman was a man and that he was in the clergy. Patrick did not have to assume that Churchman was outraged. Churchman made it perfectly clear.

Churchman: *God wills every act of sexual intercourse between husband and wife and therefore every child that results is God's creation. Scientists must leave this well alone.*
Patrick: *Man is God's partner in the art of creation, not His slave. I will not be bound to a process that fails a lot of couples. There are estimated to be 80 million men in this world with inadequate sperm or none at all.*
Churchman: *Those men have to accept what God has given them.*
Patrick: *You want to leave this suffering in the hands of the Creator. But if there is a Creator, he created cancer, malaria, viruses, earthquakes and floods. I would not leave my patients to the mercy of someone who is responsible for mass killings. Why do you think He made humans creative? So we could put right His holy work when it lets us down.*
Churchman: *Original sin makes us blind to our purpose in life and our role on His planet. God instructed us to use the Earth wisely and well. I do not classify cloning as either wise or good.*
Patrick: *What are you saying? That a cloned baby would be an abomination?*
Churchman: *No. It would be made in His image so it would not be an abomination. It would be a fully formed human with human appearance so it would not be a monster. It*

would have a soul so it would not be a mindless android. With free will, it would be answerable to God in the way it behaved. Cloning would affect the way it came into being and its physical characteristics, not the way it lives its life. On top of that, no one can blame a baby for being a clone because it did not have a choice. However, that does not make it right. You must blame the adult who made it.

Patrick: I would make it at the request of good churchgoers who are not satisfied with the sterile lives God has given them.

Churchman: Yes, people demand children obstinately and unreasonably. Fertility clinics like yours exploit that and encourage them to think children are a right rather than a blessing. You want to give your clients new life but in the process you produce lots of unwanted life – faulty embryos – and dispose of it without a thought. Then there are the still-births and deformities. Your disregard for life is your shame.

Patrick: I have not worked on humans at this stage. It is not allowed in Britain.

Churchman: But you have said you will. Besides, all creatures great and small deserve respect. The Lord God made them all.

Patrick sat back and thought about it for a moment. He was always up for a decent debate. That's why he hadn't dismissed this Churchman already. And he was always willing to justify cloning. He was almost evangelical in his desire to convert people to his own way of thinking. If he was successful with Churchman, he could convert anyone. His next message, like all of his other messages, needed to express his brash certainty and not his doubts. He smiled as he typed.

Patrick: *I remember in Genesis, God said something like, Be fruitful and multiply, and have dominion over the fish of the sea, and over the fowl of the air, and over every living thing. Also, The Lord God took one of Adam's ribs and made Woman from it. And Adam said, This is bone of my bones, and flesh of my flesh. That passage is justification enough to help people multiply, to use laboratory animals, and to clone. The Bible itself gives me the green light.*

The clinic's work was too important to be clouded by emotional responses to the need for screening. Gynaecologists would have to abort a few defective embryos and nature would reject a few more as stillbirths. That was just the way it was.

People were not like laboratory animals. The human IGF2R gene worked differently. It shouldn't switch off during cloning so it should slow down growth, making sure the foetus remained the proper size, with all its parts nicely in proportion. But Patrick was troubled. The primate IGF2R gene worked just like the human version. It shouldn't have turned off either. Yet the monkey that Patrick had just seen being dismantled like a faulty car did have overgrown organs.

Still, no matter how similar human beings were to chimpanzees, human beings were *not* chimpanzees. Maybe progress towards human cloning was too important to be stalled for much longer by a few unexpectedly bad results with monkeys.

8

Catriona was twenty-two. She was at the peak of her reproductive powers but it didn't matter. Some of her eggs had been removed by the Highpoint Fertility Clinic and kept on ice in Reprogenetics for the moment she was ready to be a mother. For now, she had a career to think of. One day, though, she'd hire an artificial womb and give her specifications for a child. That way, she would avoid the chore of pregnancy. She wouldn't risk her own health and, most important, she'd keep her figure.

Her house was crimson at the moment. When the hi-tech coating was crimson, it insulated her home. In what remained of summer, the warmth would cause the paint to change automatically to silver and cool the building by reflecting sunlight. Like the leaves that once decorated Westford, her house used to change colour with the seasons. Now, it was red most of the time and the trees had gone. Aided by the insulating form of the paint, Catriona's heating system – fuelled by the cold-fusion power station – kept the chill away. It was a pity that the authorities developed the clean source of energy too late to avoid the effects of burning fossil fuels for decades. The brakes had now been applied to global warming but it had picked up too much momentum to stop dead, and would skid out of control for years yet.

Catriona was protected from the climate. The indoor temperature was ideal for stripping off. Her bare feet nestled cosily into the soft carpet. Catriona had no need of a man for reproduction but sex was a different matter. Sex was a leisure activity for fun and exercise. With her enhanced sensory perceptions, she could enjoy it all the more. The escort she'd paid to entertain her, to provide romance, was also stripping, revealing a magnificent body. He looked every bit the expert that his upmarket agency claimed him to be. When Catriona slipped the digital watch from her wrist, her pulse was accelerating rapidly off the scale.

Afterwards, refreshed and invigorated, Catriona delved into her secret store of tobacco. Smoking cigarettes was illegal, of course. Politicians couldn't understand why any norm should be allowed to defile a perfect body. Catriona didn't smoke enough to jeopardize her unending good health. After the cloning process, when she was a mere embryo, all of the genes that might have led to cancer or heart disease in her later life had been carefully erased. Her mother was wealthy enough to buy her daughter the full range of sensory and resistance genes. There were very few diseases that could touch Catriona. She would have a long life, protected against drug addiction and almost all viruses and bacteria. She wasn't hooked on nicotine but sometimes she needed a calming drag and an element of risk.

Detecting the fumes, Catriona's housekeeper appeared almost at once. Every time Catriona let loose a narrow grey cloud into the air above the bed, the robot sterilized it with a luminous blue gas and then sucked it away. The atmosphere remained untainted.

"I'm hungry," Catriona declared. "I think I'll have . . . a delicacy. Cod with stir-fried vegetables."

The housekeeper cleaned up the ash and cigarette butt and glided silently towards the kitchen.

In a coffee bar, Myleene watched her mirror image gazing at Lights Out and edging away from Tim as if she weren't with him at all. Soon, Myleene might have to fall out with her other half over the tall asylum seeker. It was a pity that Lights Out didn't have an identical twin brother. Myleene and Anita had never really quarrelled over boys before. They got far more of a buzz from being with each other than they did from being with boyfriends so they never considered the opposite sex worthy of an argument. Maybe Lights Out would change all that.

Myleene had been winding a lock of hair round her index finger. Now, she unravelled the finger and cried in horror, "Children!"

"One day, maybe," Jordan said. "Why not?"

"How many reasons do you want? Smelly nappies, imprisonment in your own home, the cost, fishing toys out of the toilet, the noise, and for us there's the little matter of being blown up like a balloon for months on end and then being burst rather painfully."

Maynard remembered something from history. A medic once said, "The womb is a dark and dangerous place, a hazardous environment." A foetus was much safer in an artificial womb where it could be monitored and modified easily. For the women who could afford it, the artificial womb was far more popular than pregnancy. Maynard would have loved to tell Myleene how the future had taken away the labour but, of course, he did not utter a word.

"Maybe Jordan's dad could design a baby with less mess and lower running costs," Tim put in with a grin.

"How does this cloning thing work anyway?" asked Neat.

Jordan sighed. "Have you brought your toothbrush? This could take some time."

"I just don't see it. Does he have to have . . . you know . . . sperm, or what?"

Myleene's face crumpled as if she'd just got a whiff of a disgusting smell.

"No. Anything'll do. A bit of skin from the thumb is the usual," Jordan replied.

"Skin?"

"Don't they teach you anything in biology these days? Every cell in your body's got a complete set of genes. So, a skin cell's got all the information – software written in DNA – to make a whole body, but it doesn't. A skin cell stays a skin cell and doesn't become a brain cell or anything else because it's only programmed to read the bit about how to make skin. Just as well. If cells read the wrong software, you might grow a big toe on your nose. It's like a cook who's got a recipe book telling him absolutely everything he can do with an egg. Once he goes ahead and fries it, though, that's it. A one-way trip. OK? Once a nose always a nose. But cloning's different. Cloning makes it possible to go back. You can unfry your egg and start again, picking a different recipe from the book. You can reprogram the cell to build a whole new individual from a single skin cell. Easy-peasy."

Myleene muttered, "Blimey. My brain hurts. I wish I hadn't come now." She smiled at Lights Out instead.

"Dad takes a woman's egg and removes the nucleus – that's where all the genes are. Then he takes the nucleus from the donor's skin cell, pops it in the egg, turns the ignition key, and it's a result. Bob's your uncle. Or he could be your dad or your brother. It's hard to tell with cloning sometimes. Anyway, the woman's egg is only used as a pot to grow the embryo in. She doesn't supply any DNA. All that comes from the skin cell. The baby's identical to the guy who provided it."

"And the embryo thing?" Anita asked.

"It's got to go back into the woman. You need a greenhouse for your potted embryo."

"So she's got to go through a normal pregnancy? Poor thing."

"It's the usual nine months' hard labour."

"I get it," Neat said. "As far as I can see, women are vital but you could do away with men altogether. You need women for their eggs and wombs but sperm's redundant." She gave Tim a hefty nudge. "You could just clone women. We've got skin on our thumbs as well."

"That's right," Jordan admitted.

"Brilliant! That's the end of war, football, mugging, motor racing. . ."

"Yeah," said Tim, "but you'd have to live in a world where no one could throw or catch a ball properly."

"Places like China think boys are more valuable than girls so they'd only clone boys," Maynard said.

Jordan agreed. "I read about that. In the countryside,

girls in China are called 'maggots in the rice' and they abort a lot of them."

"Really?" Myleene said, appalled.

"When you get a whole truckload of clones, I wonder what you'd call them. Not twins. Sextuplets or something. Maybe polyplets or multiplets. Or just multiples." That sounded best to Jordan. Multiples were just cold numbers churned out by maths. Clones were going to be numbered babies churned out by the Finch Private Human Cloning Clinic somewhere overseas. "If you have a population of people and a society of citizens, what would you have for clones? A catastrophe of clones?"

"It'd have to be a counterfeit of clones," Tim said.

"But what if the rumours about falling sperm counts turn out to be true?" Maynard asked, taking the conversation more seriously than anyone else.

"What rumours?" said Anita.

Myleene interrupted. "We hardly know you and you're talking about sperm already. Ugh. It's gross. How on Earth did we get on to this topic?"

Ignoring her and trying hard to match the others' flippant tone, Maynard said, "Men used to have loads of the stuff but pollution's putting an end to that. They say they aren't as fertile as they used to be."

"Beats the pill or a condom, I suppose," Myleene replied.

"Well," Jordan said to Maynard, "if a lot of men become sterile, you've got a point. Cloning would crack it. But nature invented sex six hundred million years ago, according to Dad. He reckons it's about time we had a rethink. I

75

say it's done pretty well to get us this far. We can't just ditch it."

"Who cares if it's harder to get pregnant?" Myleene put in. "I'm more interested in avoiding it."

"I like babies," Lights Out pronounced, smiling as if he understood the conversation.

"I was only joking," Myleene said, reddening. "They're OK. Some time."

Tim and Neat had left. Myleene and Lights Out were trying to communicate in the corner. In a low voice, Maynard was talking to Jordan. "This is really embarrassing but . . . you know . . . I'm really worried."

"About what?"

Manipulating expertly, Maynard replied, "Infertility. Sperm counts. I mean, if you've got a problem, how would you know?"

Jordan shrugged. "See your doctor? I don't know. Get a test done, I suppose."

Maynard nodded. "I was wondering. . ."

"You want me to get you checked over at Dad's clinic!"

"Well, that'd sort it out. Hey! He could do you as well. He'd be crazy not to be worried about his own son. I bet he knows all about falling sperm counts."

Myleene raised her voice. "What are you two going on about? You look as if you're plotting a revolution."

"Nothing," Jordan replied. To Maynard, he said, "Don't hold your breath but I'll see what I can do."

The road to the clinic was blocked by seven activists.

They had handcuffed themselves to each other. Ingeniously, they'd locked hands inside barrels that were now filled with concrete. Strung across the road, the demonstration was like a ramshackle raft, made from barrels and human beings. On the grass verge, Gaia Queen gazed admiringly at Maynard – or Space Cadet as she called him. The scabs on his cheeks had gone and the scratch lines were fading. Tadpole nodded as the novice protester reported on his progress. Anti Clone merely frowned. "So, you're going to get inside – maybe," she said. "What then?"

"I've got a few options," Maynard answered, keeping it vague on purpose.

Anti Clone was not going to be impressed as easily as the other two. "Like what?" she demanded.

Police officers were lifting each demonstrator and each barrel in turn and sliding trolleys underneath them. Clearly, the police hoped to roll away the whole obstruction intact rather than attempt the difficult job of separating the linked protesters. When the demonstration began to move slowly on tiny wheels, it looked like a trick skateboard act in a circus.

Space Cadet looked from the tussle in the road to Anti Clone. "I bet you'd like some photos of deformed animal clones."

"That'd be totally great," Gaia Queen replied straight away.

"Yeah," Tadpole added. "Especially if it's a lamb, calf or a chimp. Cats and dogs are premier league as well. Rabbits are pretty good but don't bother with rats and mice. The

77

press aren't interested in rodents. For a front page splash, it's got to be cute and cuddly."

They all turned back towards the road and Gaia Queen said, "Talking of the press. . ."

Maynard spun away at once as a flurry of photographers arrived on the scene to capture the latest tactics used by both sides. Maynard also grabbed Lights Out's arm and steered him away from the cameras.

"What's wrong?" asked Gaia Queen.

Anti Clone answered for Space Cadet. "He doesn't want the Finches to see him on telly. Being seen here isn't the best way to make friends with Patrick Finch."

Tadpole took the cigarette from his lips. "Good point," he said, writing his words in the air with smoke.

Behind Lights Out and Space Cadet, the inept skateboarders were rumbling chaotically and comically down the road. There were shouts of protest, laughs, screams, and the demands of the press. The photogenic antics of SPACE City campaigners – the complete circus – would be back on the news tonight.

Lights Out smiled at his friend. "*Karosho*. Good here. Myleene good also."

That night, while Lights Out slept soundly with his feet pushed up against one end of the dome tent and his head bulging the other, Maynard listened. The earpiece whispered to him alone. Patrick Finch was on the phone, talking to a colleague about experiments with chimpanzees, the chances that human embryos would react differently to the cloning procedure, and the need to accelerate the research. Then, to conclude the conversation, Finch announced that he could use a holiday. There was a playfulness in his tone as he said, "I could book myself a few weeks in Barbados soon."

Maynard understood at once. He closed his eyes and sighed. He didn't have much time. Unknown to almost everyone, Patrick ran a small and secretive business in Barbados. The Finch Private Human Cloning Clinic wasn't in the island's phone book or advertised on the Internet but it was undoubtedly there. And history had shown that a converted plantation house in Barbados was the original source of human mutations.

The tropical island was not going to ban human cloning when its rich neighbours on either side of the Atlantic brought in dollars and pounds to set up clinics. One day, Barbados expected extra tourists as well. Already couples went there to get married, have a honeymoon and see a bit of sun in one handy package. It wasn't hard to foresee a second trip later to be cloned, see a bit more sun, and have the embryo implanted. The woman would be pregnant by the time she passed through customs again. It wouldn't be the first time that a relaxing Caribbean holiday had resulted in a baby. In a world where there'd always be some place that wouldn't criminalize human cloning, the island authorities would be fools to pass a law against it. Knowing that the cloners would always have somewhere to go, it might as well be Barbados. The tourism and tax revenue were too tempting.

If only Maynard still had his watch. With that on his wrist, he could have opened up a doorway any time and walked into the grounds of the fertility clinic instead of lying around helplessly outside it. He hadn't given up hope of finding the device. Because one day he'd want to return home, he could never afford to give up that hope. But for now, without the watch, he had to rely on Jordan Finch to access the clinic.

Maynard also faced a dilemma. His instructions were to prevent the early cloning errors, not to block successful cloning. In his time – in the future – pollution would make most men infertile and cloning was the only realistic option to continue the human race. Stopping cloning altogether could not be on Maynard's agenda. Besides, Maynard himself was a product of cloning so, if he prevented it, he would bring about his own death. And it would not just be an end to his life. He would never have existed at all. So, what was he going to do?

Murder was a simple option. Maynard didn't know if he was capable of killing one man to save the whole human race. But murder was far too simple to be a sensible solution. Even if he killed Patrick Finch, there would always be another biologist who would dare to clone humans prematurely and probably make the same mistakes – or maybe worse.

Maynard had to admit that his original orders made more sense. He had been sent back to slip the secrets of successful human cloning to Finch as unobtrusively as possible. If it hadn't been for Jordan, he would have dropped some data into a work document on Patrick's home computer on that first night, making it obvious what Finch should change to prevent genes like IGF2R from going into hibernation during the cloning procedure. That would have avoided the mutations and the holocaust released by the mutes' descendants. It would also preserve Maynard's own life.

Of course, Maynard could have written the secrets into his letter, along with the surveillance bugs, but that was hardly unobtrusive. Patrick Finch would probably have dismissed the message as attempted sabotage from an activist. A note inserted into a work file was very different. Patrick would assume it had come from one of his own workers and he would have definitely followed it up.

But, in a strange way, Maynard was pleased that he'd failed so far. He was becoming increasingly uncertain about his orders because they would bring forward a world in which people were produced in human factories and not created in human families. Out of the control of his elders, Maynard toyed instead with the idea of making the first human clone go even more spectacularly wrong. That way, he would cause a wave of revulsion that would make further experiments unacceptable, at least until every possibility of error had been eliminated.

Maynard shared some beliefs with the SPACE activists camped all around him – he pretended to share them all – but in reality his knowledge isolated him. It made his duty far more complicated and unclear. Even without the mutes, there was so much wrong with his own society. He liked the feel of this time. He liked the variety and balance among the people, the idea of families, the unpredictability of life, the notion that things were still evolving. And he liked the weather. He found himself warming easily to people with imperfections. He liked Lights Out who had the deformity of tallness and the handicap of poor hearing. He liked the natural twins with their looks that were less than the ideal. He liked Jordan Finch with the disability of short-sightedness. He liked Gaia Queen even though her brain must be faulty to make her so obsessed with animal rights. And he loved individuality. He valued that above everything else.

Again his thoughts turned to home. He had left his friends behind – the dead, the dying, and the ones who would soon be counted among the dead and dying. He missed them, even though they were all fiercely independent. If they'd been here in this time, in this culture, he could have tried to talk things through with them – just like Jordan swapped ideas with his friends. Maynard had always found it easier to control than to consult but for once he thought that he could use some opinions and advice. Even surrounded by new friends, though, Maynard was really alone. Yet inside, he felt an urge to defy his own nature and confide in someone.

18

Tadpole's cry of "SCUMBAG!" was not quite full-throated but it was fairly convincing.

As planned, none of the protesters gave the slightest hint that they recognized Space Cadet as he walked through the clinic gates with Jordan Finch under the security guards' escort. They had also hidden away Lights Out so Jordan would not spot him.

With totally believable hostility, Anti Clone spat, "BASTARDS!"

Maynard Litzoff wondered if Anti Clone had realized that his own aims and those of SPACE were not on the same wavelength. Her voice rose above the orchestrated jeers of the demonstrators.

"You don't have to worry about the ones who put themselves on display," Jordan said to him. "Barks worse than bites. They hate me but their hearts are in the right place."

A banner, thrown as a clumsy javelin, clattered on to the road just behind them.

"You don't agree with your dad's work at all, do you?"

"The world's polluted, HIV's running riot, global warming's beginning to kick in, the planet's overcrowded, and Dad chooses to clone people. There're more important – and less dangerous – things to do."

Maynard nodded. Inside, though, he was thinking about

the irony that Patrick Finch was on course to save the world from male infertility and destroy it through his mistakes. He was also going to change society for ever.

"Where do you stand?" Jordan asked, raising his voice above the din of the activists. "For or against? The other night, you were all quiet."

"You can put me down as an 'I-can-see-both-sides-of-the-argument' sort of person."

Leaving SPACE City behind, it was like entering an impregnable fortress with the drawbridge closing behind them. Jordan said, "All I know about you is, you're nice to homeless people and you want all your sperm present and correct. I had to lie to get you in. I'm not supposed to trust new friends. They're all mad bombers. You've been a mate for ages, you know."

"Thanks."

In an office of the Analysis Department, the two boys were talked through the test by a technician. "So," the young woman concluded, "I'm going to need a small semen sample from you both."

This was testing even Jordan's resistance to embarrassment. "Oh. And how are you going to get that?" He fought the impulse to squirm in his seat.

"Well, I can stick a needle where you don't want a needle stuck," she replied with a smile, "or you can go to our cubicles with a little tube and do what comes naturally – with a magazine to assist if you want. Most of our clients opt for the latter."

Bathed in soft music, sweet fragrance and subdued lighting, the cubicle was supposed to have an air of romance.

But it didn't. It felt clinical and, despite being spotless, rather dirty. The women in the magazine photos might be model females in this time but they were just normal in Maynard's. He would have been captivated more by the imperfect. Besides, for all he knew, one of the nudes could be his great-great-great-grandmother. Instead of thinking about girls, he was considering how a straightforward mission had quickly become so complicated. It should have been done in a flash on that first night. A simple correction inserted into Finch's cloning procedure, end of mission, and back home in fifteen minutes. Now, six days later, he was still here and he had even befriended the boy who had thwarted him. He was in a private cubicle in what would become Highpoint Fertility Clinic, feeling ridiculous and humiliated, trying to concentrate on an uninteresting pin-up. Just along the corridor, Patrick's son was doing the same. And on top of all that, he was having second thoughts about his mission.

To stand any chance of sorting out the fiasco, he had to relax and think about sex. He had to come up with some-thing to occupy the staff of the unit. Maynard's semen was pathetic, of course. It would not – it could not – be the stuff of new life. And sperm had played no part in Maynard's production. He had come from a clean dry skin cell and not from a sticky mess.

Jordan must also have been finding it difficult to perform to order because Maynard was first to return to the office with his sealed vial.

"Well done," the biologist said to him without a trace of awkwardness. She'd seen it all before, hundreds of times.

"That'll do fine. The big boss man told me to get a result straight away so I'll crack on. I shouldn't leave you in here on your own but as you're a friend of the family. . . You'll be OK to wait for a bit, won't you? I'm off to the lab. Room 27. You can tell Jordan to bring his sample right along."

"Yes. I'll do that."

As soon as the door closed, Maynard was behind her desk and on to her computer. Before he left his own time, Maynard had studied early twenty-first century software and knew exactly what he was doing. He delved into the Primate Trials folder and accessed the latest file that he could see. It was a detailed report on Finch's most recent failure. A chimpanzee was riddled with injuries but it died from blocked intestines, a malfunctioning liver and an enlarged heart. Maynard leaned close to the screen, scrutinizing the post mortem images of the poor creature: stretched out on its back, its skin peeled back to give an overall view of its internal organs; its liver orange and bloated; a clear picture of its intestines; several close-ups of its ballooned heart and immature lungs. The microscope shots of tissue showed enlarged blood vessels. Maynard nodded slowly. He recognized the symptoms at once. Patrick Finch had not yet brought several genes under control.

Maynard knew exactly how to accomplish his task. He could add an anonymous note to the report. He could hint at what had gone wrong. He could make suggestions that would steer future work in the right direction and lead to the elimination of the problems. Finch would be curious about which researcher had written the note but he would care more about trying out the ideas and getting a fix in place. Maynard could even tweak the experimental procedure himself.

At that moment, Maynard had the opportunity to save humankind, to save billions of people. It would take just a few minutes to plant the ideas in the computer. From Maynard's perspective, it made complete sense to give human cloning a helping hand. Reproductive cloning had to happen to avert a crisis when men became infertile. Using his knowledge of advanced reprogenetics, a discreet intervention now would put the science straight, eliminate the cruelty of mutations and save an entire population. Yet he was hesitating. Why? What could possibly overrule his orders? . . .He was thinking of the irreversible effects on society, the collapse of community. He was thinking of the inhumanity of human cloning. Paralysed, his fingers hovered over the antique keypad but he did not tap out a single word.

The moment passed. Maynard's chance to be a hero faded away when, once again, Jordan Finch intruded. Vial in hand and happy smirk on his face, Jordan appeared at the office door. When he saw Maynard at the computer terminal, his expression changed to puzzlement and he cried, "What are you doing?"

Maynard did not have a convincing reply. Still stunned by his own inability to act, he didn't even have a weak reply. He had just condemned the entire human race.

Coming up behind Maynard, Jordan saw the picture of the dead chimpanzee and winced. "Ugh!" Then, tearing his eyes from the ugly image, he stared at Maynard. "You're one of them!"

"What?"

"You're not here for . . . you know." He held up the vial. "You're a protester." For a few seconds, he studied Maynard's handsome face, the faint marks of healed scratches, the breadth of his shoulders. "Hang on. I know you. You're PP! The Polite Protester."

Emerging from his reverie, Maynard said, "Am I?"

"The name of the first person to do something is always linked with the teething troubles. Or something like that. That's what you wrote, isn't it? Now you're looking for proof of the teething troubles."

"Jordan," Maynard said softly, "we need to talk."

"Not here."

"No."

"So," Jordan said, nodding at the printer, "press *Print* and let's get going."

"Print?"

"Yes," Jordan whispered, looking round at the door to make sure they were still alone.

"Are you sure?"

"Certain."

"Your father won't. . ."

"Do it. Before anyone comes back."

"All right," Maynard agreed. "You can stall her by taking your sample to Room 27. I'll print this out."

"It's a deal."

The tests did not take long. After all, the technician had only to gaze at the sperm through a microscope, do a count and check that they were healthy swimmers. The two boys waited in a small meeting room.

Patrick had promised his son that he would deliver the results in person but it turned out to be his assistant. She did not show a trace of shame as she announced, "I'm sorry but your dad's too busy at the moment, Jordan, so he can't. . . Anyway, he asked me to have a word about your results." She was showing a trace of annoyance as if Patrick had dumped a rotten job on her. "Let me say first, everything's fine, Jordan. Well within normal range. No worries." Softening her peeved expression as much as she could, she turned to Maynard. "As far as you're concerned, Maynard, I do have some worries about your results. They're preliminary, of course, so you need to get them checked. According to us, your sperm count is lower than the average. Considerably lower, I'm afraid. Now, you understand, we're a private company so we can't carry on offering you our services but I do recommend you go and see your GP to follow this up. There may be nothing to worry about – maybe there was a mistake somewhere – but you really ought to have a thorough check-up. Don't go away and forget about it. Get an appointment straight away. That's my advice. Take it seriously. All right?"

Aghast, Jordan looked into Maynard's face. Yet his new friend was not as profoundly shell-shocked as he expected him to be.

Putting on a brave face, Maynard replied, "Yes. Thanks. I'll do that."

Once they'd left both the clinic and SPACE City behind, Jordan stopped walking. He was bemused. "What's going on?" he demanded to know.

Maynard also halted. "What do you mean?"

"You didn't ask a single question after she as good as said you're infertile. You already knew, didn't you?"

"Yes."

"You've already had the test done."

"Yes."

Jordan nodded. "It was just a trick to get into Dad's clinic and get the pictures." He tapped his school bag where they had concealed the hard copy. "You *used* me."

Maynard didn't answer.

"Where are we going to talk? Your house must be around here somewhere."

"You walked right through it."

"Uh?"

"I'm with SPACE. Sort of."

Jordan shook his head and curled his lip. "Isn't it time you came clean with me?"

"Yes, it is."

"Let's get a drink."

For a while, they walked to the town centre in silence. Then, still puzzled, Jordan said, "You're with SPACE, you wrote a protest letter to my dad, you tried to get into my house. You might be able to see both sides of the argument, but you're anti. You must be. But . . . if you can't have kids, why? Cloning's a good thing for you."

Maynard replied, "I'm not really against it. It's not as simple as being for or against. It's a tough one to call. There's a lot of issues. But I do think life's more precious without it. Once you start cloning, anyone becomes replaceable in a way."

90

"All the king's horses and all the king's men *can* put Humpty Dumpty together again."

"Eh?"

"Never mind. I know what you're saying."

"There are two problems. First, there's safety. At the moment, it's too risky to clone people. The animal experiments tell you that. The chimpanzee photos in your bag show exactly what could happen to humans. Right now, your dad's failure rate is ninety-seven per cent. Ninety seven! That's bad enough with rats or monkeys. Just imagine it with people. Your dad's jumping the gun."

"He says he's got his screening."

"I know it, but there'd still be havoc. He can abort malformed foetuses, for sure. There'll be lots of miscarriages as well, but some mistakes will get through. Some will look normal – probably – but appearances are deceptive. They could be ticking timebombs, waiting to go wrong at some stage, like the chimp. And there'll be mistakes that definitely don't look normal. Deformed babies, lots of mutants."

"Second problem?"

Maynard was choosing his words carefully. He was trying to appear well informed and reasonably far-sighted rather than far-fetched and clairvoyant. He couldn't give too much detail without arousing suspicion. He would have liked to have revealed his true origin to Jordan but he was sure that he shouldn't. "Well, I guess one day someone'll tame the science and cloning'll be safe. Will that make it OK? It might. In special circumstances." He glanced at Jordan. "Like you said, if a man can't have kids, it's a way out. If lots of men were sterile at some point in the future, that's even more reason to clone. But only when the science is ready. Rush at it now, when it's still the dark ages, and . . . disaster. But the second thing's not to do with science, genetics and all that. It's to do with people. Just imagine what a future society would be like if cloning was the way it went. It's not a pretty picture."

They went into the café, bought their drinks, sat down and carried on talking. "Not a pretty picture? How do you mean?" asked Jordan.

Maynard shrugged. "I'm not certain – who could be? – but you can guess some nightmare scenarios."

"Like?"

"Well, who do you think'll get cloned? The disabled, the poor, people with weird ideas, the unattractive, rebels, the stupid? No chance. The people they'll clone will be rich, physically perfect, beautiful and clever. All the girls will look like playmate of the month."

"There are compensations then."

"Seriously," Maynard said.

"Yeah, I know. I hear what you're saying. It'd be just people of the right type. Or someone's *idea* of what's the right type."

"Yeah. In the long run, your genetic diversity goes out the window. Everyone looks just great. That's boring and dangerous. Without variation, if there's a bug – something like botulism or a new strain of flu – and someone succumbs to it, just about everyone else will as well. On top of that, you'd get another type of imbalance."

Jordan interrupted him. "Yeah. You said. Some people'll only clone boys."

"That's right."

"I suppose, without blending two people's genes – without sex – evolution would just stop."

"Society would certainly get stuck in a rut. And family life wouldn't stand a chance. There wouldn't be any glue keeping it together. A clone's just one person's child so there wouldn't be a shared duty to bring up the children."

Jordan thought about his own dad and muttered, "Not much change there, then."

Maynard felt frustrated with Jordan Finch. This boy from the twenty-first century could not take on the magnitude of what Maynard was saying. He was considering only himself and his immediate family. Yet Maynard could not blurt out the whole truth. "You've got a father who cares about you."

"I have?"

Maynard tried not to lose his temper. "At least you've got someone to grumble about."

Sensing that Maynard was getting touchy, Jordan changed the subject. "You've really thought this through, haven't you? And you're right: it's not pretty. You're telling me Dad's even more of a menace than I thought."

"Which reminds me," Maynard said thoughtfully. "As soon as you agreed to come away with those pictures of the dead monkey, you cheated on your dad. Why?"

Jordan replied, "You said it – because what he's doing is horrible. Because he's so sure he's right, the good guy. But if everyone saw a messed-up monkey on the front page, there'd be an outcry. They'd see a chimp and imagine a dead baby. End of cloning. Just like that." It was *one* reason why he had cheated on his dad. It wasn't the main reason but he kept that to himself.

"I bet your dad's doing it with the best of intentions."

Jordan took a long cool drink. "True. But he's not driven by science and common sense. He's addicted to the idea of being first. The first person to clone a whole human being. That's his way of making himself immortal – making his name live on. But he doesn't know the difference between being famous and being infamous."

"He's really trying to help infertile couples, though. People like me owe him. He's sincere in what he believes."

Jordan agreed but he wasn't ready to admit it aloud. "I reckon, if the justification for cloning is the possibility that men might end up firing blanks, it'd be better to do something about the pollution that's causing it. That'd get rid of the problem – much better than letting it happen and then using cloning to treat the symptoms. Stop the pollution *and* human cloning. That's my solution."

For a moment, Maynard paused. He finished his Tango and then said, "Good idea. But not easy."

11

Jordan remembered a time when he used to try to influence the world by counting backwards. When he was little and eager for his dad to come home, he'd use his will power and start a countdown at ten. "Ten and nine and eight and seven. . ." Like a space rocket igniting to order, his father was supposed to appear when he got to zero. Of course, nothing happened. His dad was too busy to get home promptly, to take him to the park or the pictures or a party. Once, though, just once, it worked. At the precise moment that Jordan's ten seconds expired, his dad slotted his key into the front door. He'd managed to get back early. That was because it was Gwen's birthday.

That one success, all those years ago when he was tiny, had conditioned Jordan to think that it might magically work again. Sometimes, if he was waiting for a long overdue bus to arrive or a new girlfriend to call and he was getting desperate, he would count down silently in his head. It was silly and futile, of course, but it passed the time and it was a way of staying optimistic. While he counted down, there was always the feeling that something was about to happen.

Now, he tried it again. He was no longer young. He no longer looked forward to his dad's return each day. But tonight, while he helped his mum prepare dinner, he really hoped that his dad would appear. No matter how many countdowns he tried, though, the front door remained stubbornly shut when he reached zero.

Jordan and his mum had long since eaten when Patrick finally got home, exhausted from a busy day at work. "Phew. Sorry I'm late. Hectic isn't the word." He kissed Gwen, put his briefcase down, took off his coat and slumped into a chair. He said to Jordan, "I heard you kept your appointment."

Jordan nodded.

"Did the sperm test go all right?"

Jordan was disappointed, but not surprised, that his dad hadn't asked for the results before he left the clinic. "Yes. I'm all there. In fact, I was off the scale. Girls can get pregnant by shaking hands with me."

Patrick was too tired to laugh. "Let's hope not."

Jordan noted that he didn't enquire about Maynard's result. He might well have forgotten that Jordan had taken a friend. Jordan's exploits were nothing compared with Patrick's grand purpose in life.

Gwen carried through his dinner, resurrected by microwave like aged genes rejuvenated by pulses of electricity.

"I've got some biology homework, Dad. It's a bit tricky but it'd be a doddle for you."

His dad groaned softly but audibly. "Not while I'm eating."

Gwen said, "Your dad's been doing biology all day. Don't you think he deserves a break at home?"

Jordan loved his dad but loathed his house rules.

Jordan admired the scientist but rejected his science. Jordan loved his mum but hated the way she always, unquestioningly, supported his dad. It was only trivial little things that ever put the two of them at odds. Jordan never understood the stupid fuss about little things, and he disagreed with them over the big things. Particularly the one big thing: cloning. "I don't want him to do the work for me," he said to his mum. "Dad, I just want a push in the right direction."

"I'm afraid I've got a briefcase full of reading for tomorrow and I've got to talk through something important with a chap in the Caribbean. That'll be a long call. Let's see if there's time after that." He tucked into his meal.

"It's for tomorrow. By the time you're ready, it'll be too late for me to finish it off."

"I'm really sorry, Jordan, but you're a bright boy. I'm sure you can figure it out."

Jordan didn't pursue it. Besides, he wasn't stuck over any homework. Unbeknown to his father, Jordan had just put him through a test and he had failed miserably. Zero out of ten. Now, Jordan knew exactly what he would do with the pictures of the chimpanzee. "How are your latest clones?" he asked. "Thriving?"

Patrick perked up. "Mixed. Some good results, some not so good."

Presumably, Jordan thought, his dad was categorizing the death of the monkey among the not-so-good. The chimp would probably have agreed. "You know, if you get it right with people, they'll lay into you for playing God. If it goes pear-shaped – if the first baby's got some horrible defect – you'll be branded a monster. Frankenstein'll have nothing on you. You're not going to win either way."

Patrick chewed a piece of meat and swallowed it as quickly as he could. Impatiently, he retorted, "It doesn't matter about me. The point is, a childless couple'll win. It's not about me winning."

"Isn't it?" Jordan's blood was up now. "I reckon if you weren't blinded by the race, you wouldn't dare do it. Don't medical ethics say you can only do something if it's safe? You shouldn't clone anyone if the chances of getting birth defects are worse than a normal pregnancy."

Animated, Patrick waved his knife towards Jordan. "If I don't do it, someone else will. Some scientists and some companies will do anything for money and some people who can't have children will pay anything to get their own child. There's no point resisting something that's inevitable. I think King Canute proved that ages ago. And I won't be preached at by. . ."

Jordan got up and stormed out.

In his bedroom, Jordan fiddled some more with the hi-tech watch. It was no longer working because, by trial and error, he had removed various units until the face went blank. He knew then that he had the power source in his hand. It was a tiny metallic cube, apparently sealed, with electrical contacts on opposite sides. It was nothing like a conventional battery and inside the watch it was placed where the sun never shone so it wasn't a solar cell.

Jordan looked at the power source under a magnifying glass and shook his head. If the watch belonged to Maynard Litzoff, if he had lost it when he'd made a dash through the hedge, he was not going to be happy when Jordan finally admitted that he'd experimented on it till it was as dead and mangled as the cloned chimp.

For an instant, Jordan had an utterly mad idea. A ridiculous idea. An idea as daft as willing something to happen by counting down to zero. But it made a perverse sense. The mechanism of the watch was from a different world. The date in one of its displays, when it still worked, was way into the future. Maynard had an uncanny ability to predict what might happen. He said that men could become infertile in the future and his own sperm count was pitiful.

No. The idea was too crazy.

Gwen had four jobs. She was a part-time librarian, she looked after the family's security, and she was a wife and mother. Patrick had only one job: biologist.

She was lying next to a remarkable man. In the darkness, she could barely see him but she could hear him. He didn't snore exactly. The intermittent sound was a hybrid of snoring and breathing. It was not just familiar but reassuring. At the library she worked all day with famous names, written on book spines. Tonight and every night she lay down with someone who would dwarf them all. She was immensely proud of him, of course, she would help him every step of the way, but she did not feel as fulfilled as she should.

Once, Gwen would have opted for a second child – a girl, a sister for Jordan – but one baby was quite enough for Patrick. Truth be told, he had not made a good father but perhaps great men never did. They were too wrapped up in their calling to take on the extra jobs of husband and father. It wouldn't have been fair on either Patrick or the baby to bring another into the world.

Patrick's rasping breath ended in a grunt. He turned over and opened his eyes. Only the whites showed up. "Can't sleep?"

"It's nothing."

"It's never nothing."

"Well, since you asked," Gwen whispered, "I don't think it would've killed you to help Jordan."

Patrick sighed. "I was tired. I'm still tired."

"It's OK to help other men to be fathers but you've got to be one yourself."

Patrick rolled over again, muttering, "Don't remind me about my failings now, Gwen. I already know. Perhaps when I've got the next few experiments under my belt. . ."

"Yeah." As always, Gwen let him off the hook. She let him slip back into sleep.

She had her reservations about cloning but she never voiced them. It struck her that, when Patrick was sure it was safe to clone humans, there was an obvious way she could be certain of having a daughter and certain of Patrick's interest in the girl.

12

The road outside the Finch Private Fertility Clinic marked the boundary of SPACE City. In the first light of morning, the police had arrived at the scene once more because there was another disturbance of the peace and the highway had been obstructed yet again. A little way down the lane, out of range of Finch's guards and the spotlights, SPACE had erected a substantial wall under the cover of darkness. Led by the two activists who had once infiltrated the construction company and learned all about bricklaying, the demonstrators had built a wall right across the road in the night. Now, while the protesters, police and security guards waited for a bulldozer to arrive, tempers were getting frayed.

There was even tension within the encampment. Anti Clone was almost shouting at Space Cadet. "You should have given us the pictures!"

"Why?" Maynard asked.

"You gave them straight to the enemy." She shook her head in disbelief.

"Jordan Finch isn't the enemy and he'll know what to do with them."

"Like, destroy them?"

"I doubt it. He agreed to me taking them."

"How do we know you're not making all this up?" Anti

101

Clone said heatedly. "How do we know you got any pictures?"

"That's totally out—" Gaia Queen began to object.

Maynard did not need her defence. "You'll know it when Jordan does something with them."

"SPACE should be doing it. We've got the experience. We're the official resistance."

Maynard needed no further evidence of Anti Clone's competitiveness. If there was going to be a public outcry, she wanted the glory. He argued, "Surely it doesn't matter who stops Finch, as long as someone does."

Tadpole said, "It might be even more powerful if everyone knew it came from within his own family."

"If he does anything," Anti Clone retorted, "he'll do it anonymously. Guarantee it."

Suddenly, Lights Out looked up and grinned.

Maynard turned to see the source of his pleasure. It was one of the twins.

Cowering under a hood, looking shifty and nervous, she walked over to them. "How you doing?" She looked at Lights Out and Maynard.

"*Karosho*. Good," said Lights Out.

"In case you're wondering, I'm Myleene."

From the other direction, some security guards were urging the small group to move back from the edge of the road.

"What are you doing here?" Maynard asked her.

"Jordan said you'd be here. He wants to see you but can't risk coming himself." She glanced round. "I'm not sure about me, either. Anyway, I volunteered."

"What's it all about?"

"No idea," Myleene answered. "He's always been the hush-hush James-Bond type. Because of all this."

The guards, instead of just shooing them away, began to push. Myleene had her back towards them and didn't see it coming. She cried out in shock and turned on the nearest security officer. At once, the two of them started grappling with each other. She screamed and began to hit out blindly in panic.

Lights Out was appalled. In his eyes, it was wrong and unfair for a beefy male guard to pick on a girl. Chivalrously, he went to her aid. Without another thought, he walloped the security officer. It was a single clean punch, neatly avoiding Myleene but felling the man instantly. He was out cold before he flopped on to the ground.

Immediately, there was chaos. Protesters, guards, police.

Anti Clone was an old hand at this game. She grabbed Lights Out and bundled him away from the scuffle before he could be arrested. As she did so, she muttered, "I thought you were just a big softie. But no. You're talking my language all of a sudden. I understand the Lights Out bit now."

"Myleene," Lights Out muttered, trying to go back into the fray.

Anti Clone resisted. "She'll be fine. I've got to hide you before the cops get hold of you."

Back in the scrum, a policewoman clutched Myleene's arm and began to drag her away. But, halfway across the road, the hood fell back from the writhing suspect and the officer cried, "Myleene!"

Myleene reddened. "Mum!"

"What's. . .?"

"Oh, no," Myleene groaned.

"What do you think you're doing?"

"It's . . . er. . . It's a long story," Myleene replied.

The rest of the group calmed down to watch the unlikely pair. The exchange between mother and daughter was defusing the whole situation. There was even some quiet laughter.

"What are you doing here?"

"I'm not," Myleene replied. Looking foolish, she said, "I mean, I'm only here to see someone. It's all a . . . you know . . . nothing."

"Nothing! You're lucky I don't have to arrest you. Who was that tall lad who threw the punch?"

Myleene shrugged.

"Where is he?"

"No idea. Looks like he's gone. But he was just trying to protect me."

"Mmm." Myleene's mum shouted to everyone: "All right. Let's just cool it and we won't have to take this any further." Quoting the official line, she said, "Peaceful protest's OK but we can't tolerate anyone who stops others going about their legitimate business. And we won't tolerate violence." To her daughter, she added quietly but threateningly, "I'll see you at home."

"Sorry, Mum."

Down the lane, the sturdy wall was no match for an ugly bulldozer. Bricks and mortar crashed noisily to the tarmac as the massive machine rumbled into the obstruction.

As soon as Myleene had arranged a meeting between Maynard and Jordan, she scurried away. She was so unnerved that she didn't even wait to see Lights Out again.

From the side, the grey concrete formed a giant U. Boys on bikes and skateboards started at the top of one of the man-made mini-mountains, plunged down and then flew up the other side. The real experts on bikes took off, twisted their handlebars, turned acrobatically in mid-air, and landed neatly on the steep slope to begin again. Underneath the helmets and all-over safety clothing, it was difficult to iden-tify individual riders. It would have been hard to tell a boy from a girl but almost all of them were boys anyway. With so much of themselves covered, they looked like camou-flaged cloning protesters. All in much the same standard protective gear, doing much the same thing, they also looked like clones.

The young audience watched, sometimes groaned as a cyclist hit the deck, sometimes cheered when a clever manoeuvre was executed perfectly. Yet not everyone in the Leisure Centre paid attention. Myleene had gone off some-where with Lights Out. Jordan and Maynard were whis-pering secrets together.

Jordan held out a folded A4 envelope. "Here's a photo-copy. It's the one that shows all the monkey's innards. Really hideous. Anyway, here's the idea. You write one of your polite letters to go with it, telling Dad to stop cloning or all the prints go to the press. People would choke on their cornflakes to see a chimpanzee cut open on the front page. The animal rights brigade would hit the roof."

Maynard looked doubtful. "It might be pointless. Will your dad take any notice?"

"The tabloids are very imaginative. Give them these pictures and they'll report all sorts. Not just a dead cloned monkey. Not just malformed hearts and livers. They'll dream up two-headed lambs or whatever. Before long, they'll have everyone believing that cloning'll make two-headed babies."

"Maybe," Maynard replied. He was thinking that, if things got too hot for Patrick Finch in England, he'd just go underground in Barbados. After all, last night Finch had made the final arrangements by telephone for a trip to the Caribbean. Yet Maynard couldn't tell Jordan that. He still couldn't run the risk of appearing to be too well informed.

"Just make sure you don't leave any hair or tiny flakes of skin on the paper or lick the stamp," Jordan advised him. "They'll get a DNA sample and identify you."

"I know it. But I'm not in their database."

"Not with a name, no. But Forensics got your DNA from the bush in our garden so, if you give them another sample, they'll know who they're looking for."

Maynard remained silent, thoughtful.

"What's wrong?" Jordan asked.

"It's just that. . . Well, let's hope no one makes the connection."

"What connection?"

"Think about it. Your dad's got a sample from me at the clinic. And he's got my name."

Jordan swore, hesitated and then said, "Well, we've just

got to hope the forensic people don't link up with the fertility clinic."

"If they do, it'll lead to you as well," Maynard said gravely. "You can plead innocence – say you didn't know what I was up to – but you took me to the clinic. They'll guess I stole the pictures. That technician will admit she left me alone in a room with a computer terminal. She'll say she trusted me because I was with you."

Jordan shivered. He intended to threaten his father but now, for the first time, he realized that he could become the one who was threatened. The only safe thing to do was to destroy the pictures and forget all about his plan. But he wasn't prepared to do that. Someone who faced bomb threats and verbal abuse every day did not give up so easily. "Don't worry about me," he replied. "Just get on with it."

Maynard could see that Jordan was tenacious. He had probably inherited determination from his dad. Patrick Finch would not bow to pressure either. Finch Senior wouldn't halt his research programme because he was being blackmailed. "You could just send the pictures to the newspapers straight away." Maynard was thinking of his second plan: causing a wave of revulsion that would delay human cloning until it was reliable and harmless.

"Maynard?"

"What?"

"Who are you? Why are you so sure your name's not in their database?"

"I haven't got involved before," Maynard answered.

"Yeah. That's what I thought. Where do you come from?"

"What do you mean?"

"Where do you come from?" Jordan repeated.

"Westford."

Jordan nodded. For a few seconds he watched the lads on wheels zooming down, levelling off, letting their momentum carry them up the opposite slope. It was a game, an opportunity for the riders to show off, and a physics lesson rolled into one. It was all about gravity, friction, balance, potential energy, kinetic energy. Jordan took a deep breath and looked into Maynard's face. "OK. *When* do you come from?"

There was an abrupt and complete change in Maynard. He grabbed Jordan's arm and turned him away from the crowd. "What do you mean?" he whispered urgently.

"I mean what I said. When do you come from? Though I think I can guess."

"What are you talking about?"

Jordan thought for a moment. "I'm talking about the distant future, I suppose."

"That's crazy."

"Yes. I thought so. But your reaction. . . Makes you think, doesn't it? After all, what's time? It's just nature's way of stopping everything happening at once. Perhaps it can be bypassed."

Behind them, there was a big cheer as a cyclist pulled off a particularly difficult and hazardous trick.

"Listen to what you're saying. It's ridiculous." The necessity for absolute secrecy had been ingrained in Maynard. But so had a loathing for imperfection and yet, here he was, not just associating with it in the twenty-first century, but enjoying it.

108

"You're resorting to clichés. That means you're lying."

"Why do you think I'm from the future?"

"Lots of things. You're not on databases, you've got remarkable foresight, you're infertile like men in the future will be – according to you. And you're not denying it strongly enough." Jordan was too embarrassed to mention the futuristic watch because he had dismantled and damaged it beyond repair. "You've come back to stop Dad, haven't you? There's going to be some disaster."

"If I'm from the future, from infertile stock, I must be a clone. So, would I campaign against cloning? That's like you trying to ban sex between would-be parents. If you're right and I stop cloning, I kill myself." He shrugged as if at a silly idea.

Jordan would not be sidetracked. "You're on a suicide mission. It wouldn't be the first time someone's sacrificed themselves for a cause. It was in a *Star Trek* film. The good of the many outweighs the needs of the one. Or something like that. Then Spock saved them all by dying."

"Sorry but . . . what are you talking about?"

"That clinches it. If you don't know about *Star Trek*, you're either from another planet or another time. You don't look like an alien so. . ."

They sat down on a bench. In front of them, airborne cyclists bobbed up regularly and then plummeted out of view.

"What if I admitted it?" Maynard said. "I could be having fun at your expense."

"Yeah. You could. But I don't think you would."

Every last molecule of his body told him to dismiss

Jordan's notion as plain silly. Every part of his training told him to deny it. Yet he wanted to ignore all his instincts and talk openly with this boy. After all, his elders were a long way away and unable to reach him. Even if some of them were still alive, only one watch like his had ever been made. It was unique, attuned only to him. He hung his head and then, more resolute, looked up. "In my day, your dad's place is called the Highpoint Fertility Clinic. The pinnacle of good breeding."

"Yes!" Jordan cried. "Result!"

"What? I didn't think you'd celebrate—"

Jordan interrupted. "No. It's not every day you meet someone from another time. Well, *you* do, of course, but. . ." Jordan shook his head. "I'm getting all tongue-tied. Sorry. I was celebrating getting you to admit it. It's amazing. And you're a clone!"

Maynard looked round to make sure no one was within listening distance. "A perfectly healthy clone. The emphasis on perfect. It's not all bloated hearts and tongues, squashed faces and two-headed sheep. In fact, it's never been two-headed sheep. First, they made cloning safe. Then, when men became more and more infertile, it shifted from being an unpopular IVF service to an essential one."

"Wow. Perfect, eh? Don't people get ill or disabled? Or do you just cure things like cancer? Just like that. No problem."

Maynard tried to rein in Jordan's galloping imagination. "We're pretty hopeless at curing things, actually. It's a lack of practice because there's not much need. We just prevent

110

most illnesses happening in the first place. Plucking bad genes out before the cloning process takes care of heart disease and cancer. To beat viruses and bacteria – most of them anyway – we add good genes. Take AIDS. Right now, in your time, about one per cent of the world's got natural resistance to the virus. In the future, they'll just share that resistance gene with the rest of us and so no one will get AIDS. All very straightforward. Most norms – they're ordinary clones – can afford to have gene surgery on their embryos. That way, their children just don't get ill."

"It's more than cloning, then. It's genetic engineering – designer babies – as well."

"Reprogenetics, it's called. It started because everyone wanted to see an end to the big killers: malaria, cancer, heart disease, AIDS. Then it spread to diabetes, asthma, poor eyesight and hearing, tooth decay, depression, hair loss, and that sort of thing. Before long, people were demanding artificial genes that made their clones stronger, faster, more intelligent, better-looking, more musical or artistic. You could even add animal genes if you wanted. No one could draw a clear line between cracking disease and designer babies so it became a free for all. The marketplace rules. Besides, every parent wants the best for their child. There's gene packs, straight off the shelf. I suppose, in a funny way, evolution isn't dead," Maynard said. "It's just not left to chance any more. You see, when people talk about making copies today, they're thinking about your photocopy devices. The copy you get isn't as good as the original because there's a loss of quality. Cloning's not like that. The copy's better than the original because faulty genes are removed and a package of good genes gets put in. Then, by the time that generation of enhanced norms want children of their own, reprogenetics has moved on and a fresh batch of gene enhancements comes on stream. The next norms are even more enhanced. That's a new sort of evolution in quantum leaps. Athletes are doing a hundred metres in under seven seconds and someone'll do it in six soon."

"This is. . . Wow. And you're saying people aren't short-sighted?"

"As long as they can afford the right package, they won't be short-sighted, fat or deaf, they won't have learning difficulties. They just don't happen now . . . I mean, then. In the future."

"And what about those who can't afford it?"

Maynard did not like the question. He shuffled uncomfortably, so ashamed of the answer that he didn't give it. "There's a few germs that the scientists never developed a resistance gene for. Like the common cold. And the botulism bacteria. Hardly anyone escapes the toxin it produces." He looked distracted, his eyes returning to the concrete curves.

Jordan fingered his glasses. "No specs," he muttered to himself, engrossed by a notion that meant a lot to him. "Sounds great. Life's never been fair to people with glasses. You only have to watch telly or a film. Glasses are a cheap prop that shouts, 'This person is studious, amazingly unsexy and unspeakably ugly!' Then there's the stupid Superman transformation. When someone takes their specs off, they're automatically transformed into a sex bomb ready to go off at any second. Glasses on: incredibly dull. Glasses off: horizontal tango imminent."

Maynard looked bemused at Jordan's rant. It was all outside of his experience.

Jordan asked, "Do people still have sex?"

"Yes. It's just that clones have separated the urge for sex from the urge to reproduce. Sex is a pastime, reprogenetics is for reproduction."

"How did you get here?"

"To your time?"

"Yes."

"I. . ." Maynard hesitated. He'd been sworn to secrecy over his watch and he certainly didn't want to admit he'd been careless enough to lose it. "I had a device."

"I can't take all this in," Jordan said. "I've got a million and four questions. But, just tell me this. What's the disaster? What have you come back for?"

13

The receptionist at the Leisure Dome looked up at Catriona and David. "Swipe, please," she said.

The young Catriona had learnt all about swiping. The subcutaneous disc in her palm held an electronic record of everything there was to know about her. She brushed her hand over the reader and immediately her details came up on the screen. She was a Class A clone, one of the genetic aristocracy, with every improvement available seven years ago when she was born.

"Fine," the receptionist said, glancing at her file. "Come in and enjoy the centre."

David followed suit.

This time, the receptionist's face fell. David was Class C, no enhancements at all. He was merely a replica of his parent. As a primitive who had not evolved, the boy was a medical liability. He was not a danger to protected children like Catriona but he could be carrying diseases that would be transmitted to other unenhanced children if they were allowed in. To treat all Class C clones equally, the centre kept them all out. "Sorry," the attendant said. "No Class Cs."

Devastated, David crumpled visibly. He'd been shamed in front of Catriona.

Catriona was astonished. With a wicked smile, she cried,

114

"Class C! You're so poor you're almost a mute." Then she skipped happily into the Leisure Dome.

Some of the underground service ducts into the Leisure Dome were enormous, easily big enough for a gathering of mutes.

Fascinated, Zadie listened carefully to the adults. At the age of seven, though, she did not understand a lot of what they said. Usually it was because of the words they used – words like inherited metabolic disorders, learning difficulties, infant mortality, thalassaemia – and sometimes it was because of the speakers' misshapen mouths.

"We were cloning cast-offs and we've been ostracized by society," Zadie's mother yelled. "They're not going to help us or make amends. They wish we didn't exist. It's time for revenge – for justice."

"No, not yet," the woman at the front replied. "We're not ready."

"We could sabotage these pipes," someone else suggested.

"And spoil a child's day out. Maybe even kill a few children. What's the point? They can make new children."

The group was the usual mishmash of mutes. The physically disabled sat in the grime, reliant on family, friends or makeshift wheelchairs to carry them from place to place. The blind ones clung to their fellows. Many, with the most severe learning disorders, understood less than Zadie. A few of the mutes panted continuously as if they were constantly recovering from a long exhausting run. Some were totally deaf but stood there as a matter of support. Besides, they hadn't got anything better to do.

115

None of the mutes ever had anything to do except survive.

"Their babies live, ours die."

"The norms catch nowt. Cancer, heart attacks, germs. Nowt. They're OK. We get everything. It's not fair. I can barely hear owt, see owt."

"At least you can use your arms and legs." The man who said it had a cumbersome mouth that turned all his *s* sounds into *sh*.

In a meeting like this, the only mutes to be heard were the ones who could speak in a loud and clear voice. Many did not express their opinions because they couldn't. Some were badly retarded and others were choked by a mouthful of outsize tongue. One man standing close to Zadie – occasionally leering at her, weighing her up for future use – had a tongue so large that it hung from his mouth like a dog's and rested on his chin.

The early failures in human cloning propagated themselves through sex. Yet few could actually create children. Those who could produced children with ever more weaknesses. Each new generation carried the legacy of bad cloning methods and the chronic diseases of inbreeding. Each new generation was inferior to the one before.

"And look at their houses, their schools!"

The leader had heard enough. "And look at their capabilities," she yelled. "If we make a nuisance of ourselves, they've got enough technology to wipe us from the face of the planet. You know this. They know it. They know our genetic weak spots. They could easily design a biological weapon to kill us all off. Morals and embarrassment hold them back. Let's not give the norms an excuse to abandon those morals."

116

Zadie's mum drew her child aside from the ragbag collection and whispered, "They're not going to do anything. Again. But one day they will, Zadie. I tell you. They'll see sense one day. Then they'll have to strike hard before the norms can wipe us out. You've got to be ready for that day."

"Yes, Mum," said Zadie obediently.

"I won't live much longer. Promise me you'll remember. Promise me you'll do your duty when the time comes."

The girl did not understand but again she replied, "Yes, Mum."

14

Groups of cyclists, onlookers and lads with skateboards tucked under their arms were making their way slowly and boisterously from the Leisure Centre. Without their protective helmets and clothing, they had become individuals again.

Still sitting apart from the thinning crowd, Maynard nodded towards one young spectator. "See him? Look, he's got terrible eyesight, he's too short, doesn't look like he's got the world's best brain, and he's limping with a bad leg. Almost a mute. Even so, he's here. He's allowed in. Not in my day. A sorry specimen like him wouldn't stand a chance. His genes wouldn't be acceptable," Maynard said, sighing. "What's wrong with my world? The whole society's unfair."

"A catastrophe of clones," Jordan whispered to himself, remembering something he'd said a few days ago.

Carrying on as if he hadn't heard, Maynard said quietly, "The weather's absolutely dire as well – thanks to global warming – but really . . . it's the people. Norms. They're intolerant and intolerable. It's easy to see how it all got out of hand. Norms are perfect copies so they expect perfection in everything – the best set of genes, the best looks, the best education, the best house. And that makes them insufferable. Anyone else – a mute or a lower grade clone with no genetic modification – is seen as a defective product. Today you wouldn't put up with a new mobile phone that's defective, would you? You'd take it back and demand a perfect one. Well, the norms of the future won't tolerate anyone who's not up to their own pitch of perfection."

"Spoilt spitting images," Jordan muttered. Then he added, "I don't want to sound like some preacher but you don't have to be a brainy stunner to be a good person. A good person's a good person, irrespective. Surely, being good's the thing, not being a supermodel."

Maynard let out a long weary breath. "When a world demands flawless people, when it can deliver flawless people, there's no sympathy for the faulty, there's no humanity towards them."

"But you're different. You don't think like that."

"Don't I? I don't now, I suppose. Maybe that's one reason I was sent back — because I'm more tolerant. I don't know." He shrugged dejectedly.

"I was going to ask, 'Why you?' Are you some sort of VIP?"

Maynard laughed wryly. "No. Nothing like. Someone once looked into my bloodline. The earliest Litzoff they found was a doorman. Nothing grand, but. . ." The sadness returned to his eyes. "In my time, families don't exist."

"That could be a big plus."

"I assure you it's not," Maynard snapped.

It was plain that Maynard was not in the mood for light-heartedness. "All right. You said there were no families. Why not?"

This time, Maynard did not have to contain his frustration. He let rip. "Think about it. They're redundant. When women get themselves cloned, they don't need male partners. When the artificial womb came along, the only thing men needed from women was unfertilized eggs and you can buy them – frozen – from any clinic. You don't even have to know a woman." Maynard waited for some girls to wander past, then he carried on. "At first, some couples stuck together anyway – through choice – but the whole thing fell apart in a few years. Imagine the first child's a genetic copy of the man. *She* couldn't cope with a baby that looked nothing like her, that had nothing to do with her. No pregnancy, no chemistry between them. She couldn't develop a bond. *He* had the opposite problem: too big a bond. He'd try to get the boy to relive his own childhood. He'd feel every bit of pain his boy went through. He'd get all grumpy – and sometimes violent – if Mum told the kid off. You see, he thought of the boy as himself so, in his mind, *he* was being told off. The way he saw it, when Mum rejected the boy, she was kind of rejecting him as well. That had the family simmering. And the boy himself brought it to the boil. He was messed up. He didn't understand why Mum was distant and Dad was acting strange. He had to live in his dad's shadow and probably wasn't coming up to expectations – which were unrealistic anyway, no doubt. On top of that, he thought he could see exactly where he was heading. Just looking at Dad was like looking into his own future. Scary. So, he did weird things he didn't want to do just to steer clear of being like his dad. If Dad was the academic sort, the boy played up at school. If Dad was a big bruiser, the boy went all soft and sensitive. His urge to rebel came out all right, but it was against his own nature. So, everyone in the family got a big dose of disappointment and friction."

Jordan nodded. "Yeah. I can see that. At least I can say, 'I'm not going to grow into an ugly old git like my dad.' There'll be other genes mixed in."

"For the few families who survived all that trauma, some of them got hit by another. Sometimes a woman would fall in love with her 'son' when he got to the age of twenty, just like she fell in love with his father at the same age."

"Oops," Jordan said. "That's awkward."

"A recipe for hands-around-the-throat meltdown. The kid imploded and the family exploded. End of family – for the sake of everyone's sanity."

Jordan hesitated before facing Maynard. "It must be really scary – that's what you said – to see your future. But that's what you've done to me, Maynard. You're letting me see the future. You didn't spare my sanity."

"I know it. I didn't want to but . . . I need to know what you think."

"I don't think anything till I know what the disaster is. You've not said. It's something to do with those mutants, isn't it?"

Maynard was in too deep to clam up now. He had no choice but to tell Jordan about the terrible revenge unleashed by the mutes.

Jordan listened in stunned silence and then exclaimed, "My God! That's what my dad's about to do. He's going to make the human race extinct. No wonder you came back. We've got to stop him!"

"We?"

"Yeah," Jordan replied. "We."

"I'm used to acting alone."

"If you wanted to go it alone, why draw me into it?"

Maynard hesitated and then nodded. "All right. Here's the problem. Your dad'll make some mistakes. The first mutes. Their descendants will wipe out the human race. But your dad's got to get cloning off the ground. If he doesn't, infertility's going to wipe humanity out. We're damned if he does, damned if he doesn't."

"You could've sorted it at the clinic yesterday but you didn't. You could've put him on the right track."

"I could, but I couldn't, if you see what I mean. I couldn't set the ball rolling – not knowing how it ends up."

"When people saw how it was going, why didn't someone just outlaw it?" asked Jordan.

"Because it was necessary. Men were infertile. Anyway, politicians were all enhanced clones. Were they ever going to stop cloning? No chance."

"I guess turkeys don't vote for Christmas. But you are. You're thinking of putting a complete stop to cloning, aren't you?"

"Maybe. But that's not why I got sent back."

"You're a bit of a maverick, then. With the weight of the entire world on your shoulders."

"Sometimes it feels like that, yes."

"There's a way out," Jordan announced.

"Oh?"

"I said it before. Yesterday. We could stop work on cloning as long as we do something about pollution as well. Men won't go sterile, no need to clone."

"In theory, yes. But it's a tiny bit ambitious."

Jordan was getting more and more excited at the prospect of the challenge. And at the prospect of wrecking his dad's research. "Look, there's no point coming back to do half a job. There's nothing wrong with ambition. My mum always told me not to set myself modest targets. I bet your mum, if you'd had one, would've said the same thing. Come on. What's behind the falling sperm counts?"

"All sorts of things. They're called endocrine disrupters. Some chemicals in plastics, some pesticides, the whole way you lead your lives really, but. . ." Maynard's voice faded to nothing.

"But what?"

"Well, there was a final straw, I suppose. There's a new suntan lotion about to hit the shops. Clever marketing will make it take off in a big way. Come summer, everyone'll be using it and it'll get everywhere. Men'll be slapping huge amounts of it all over themselves, polluting their own bodies, the water they swim in and eventually the sewer system. It'll stop skin cancer but no one'll notice its side-effect of stopping sperm production as well. Not till it's too late. By then, it'll be giving Fairway Pharmaceuticals an enormous profit and they'll say, 'If there's a problem, it's for the medics to solve, not a reason for commerce to change.'"

"OK. We stop it," Jordan replied quickly.

"Easy to say. And theirs isn't the only product to blame."

"But if we stopped the prime suspect and got the press behind us, we'd get a bit of publicity for the poor old sperm and that way we'd broaden the net."

"Maybe," Maynard replied.

"More than maybe," Jordan said with determination. "It's a great plan. Block the sunscreen and block cloning. Problem solved. Result."

Myleene and Lights Out came back into the Leisure Centre. As soon as Maynard saw them, he leaned towards Jordan and whispered, "Don't tell *anyone* about me."

Jordan smiled and shook his head. "No worries about that. I don't want to be carted away to the nearest psychiatric unit."

Lights Out was striding towards them, clutching a box and beaming like a child on Christmas morning. Myleene had bought him a sandwich toaster.

15

Jordan was not asleep. Even if he had been trying to sleep, his tormented brain would not have let him. In his mind, he had an image of his dad, not just at the helm of a fertility clinic, but as captain of the *Titanic*. He was sailing confidently and blindly towards the iceberg. Every single passenger was going to go down unless Jordan could force the ship to change course.

Earlier in the evening, Jordan had even toyed with the idea of talking to his dad, trying to persuade him that he was heading for disaster. But Jordan didn't waste much time on the thought. His father would have scoffed at Jordan's ludicrous story. And if Jordan had told his dad that he really knew the future, scornful laughter would have rattled the rafters. Jordan wouldn't willingly expose himself to that sort of ridicule.

He glanced at his bedside clock. It read 00:40, approaching the time when most people entered their deepest sleep. Only twenty minutes to go before he would creep quietly out of the house under cover of darkness.

Twelve forty. Patrick was on the verge of sleep but his overactive brain – and the uncomfortable pinpricks of his conscience – would not let him slide peacefully into deep sleep. An image of his bruised and battered sister kept walking on to the dark screen created by his closed eyes.

At the age of nineteen, Patrick's big sister, Amber, had married. At the time, neither Amber nor Theo realized that Theo was infertile. For nine years, they tried for children. Theo got frustrated, Amber got impatient. Theo was adamant that he couldn't possibly be to blame. He wouldn't have his manhood called into question, so Amber went elsewhere for healthy sperm. Her unfaithfulness wasn't really an affair. It was a purely mechanical act – after all, she still loved her husband – yet she felt it was necessary because she was desperate to be a mother. Unknown to Amber, though, Theo had admitted to himself that he might have a problem. Secretly he'd had his sperm count tested and the result was lousy, absolutely lousy. He was never going to give Amber a baby. When Amber announced that she was pregnant, Theo knew that the child wasn't his. The fertility test had already damaged his self-esteem, but Amber's pregnancy damaged it a lot more.

At the age of twenty-eight, Amber came home with a black eye and a bloodied nose. Patrick was just twenty, home from university. Even now, years later, Patrick could picture his sister dissolving in tears on the doorstep, frightened, make-up running down her face, looking like a tramp who'd just been beaten up on the streets. From that point, Patrick had always known what career he would follow.

That career got one huge boost. It came when Patrick was first employed as a young researcher by the Institute for Genetic Knowledge. It came when he was too eager to wait for permission for animal cloning experiments. Under the microscope in IGK's laboratory, the empty sheep's egg looked like a barren moon waiting for a meteor strike. The ultrafine needle pushed against the magnified egg's surface, denting it, squashing it, turning it sickle-shaped, and then finally piercing it. The egg swallowed the tip of the needle and became spherical again. Carefully and skilfully, Patrick operated the plunger and the syringe delivered the genes of an adult sheep called Sarah. And there, on the end of the pipette, was the beginnings of a replica of Sarah, less than the size of a full stop, ready for electrical stimulation and insertion into Sarah's womb.

Then the permission that Patrick believed would be a formality was refused. The Committee for Animal Experiments concluded that there were too many unknowns to attempt cloning yet. It was deemed immoral and too dangerous for both the sheep and any cloned offspring. The experiment was forbidden just after Patrick confirmed that he had successfully implanted the egg and Sarah was pregnant. So the young researcher had to cover it up. He had to take the procedure forward in secret. After all, it was only a sheep and IGK was supposed to be a research institute that aimed to improve genetic knowledge. Someone had to push the boundaries. If the Institute waited until every possible danger had been eliminated from every possible experiment, there would never be any advances in genetic knowledge.

Patrick smuggled Sarah out of IGK and resigned to set up his own company. At first, it was barely more than an improvised laboratory and a field. Yet, in those makeshift conditions, Sarah gave birth to a lamb. Except that it was twisted almost beyond recognition and barely alive. What Patrick got was not Sarah Mark 2 but a cruel mockery of Sarah the sheep.

Sarah licked her newborn lamb clean and then tried to nudge the ugly creature on to its legs. At first, she did it patiently, lovingly and gently. But Sarah didn't know that the lamb had totally useless limbs. She began to nudge it more insistently, with an aggression born of increasing alarm and incomprehension. Finally, getting no response, she gave up and backed away. She rejected her offspring, with its chest blown up and stretched like a balloon, a mere parody of life. A mutation.

Patrick was delighted that Sarah 2 was alive at all. To him, she was a godsend and he adopted her straight away. Against all the odds, he kept her alive and learned a huge amount from her. Working late every night, he studied the wretched creature until he couldn't keep her going any longer. Then, he learned a whole lot more when he performed an intricate and thorough post-mortem.

From that moment, Patrick became an expert in cloning techniques, way ahead of the pack, but he had to keep quiet about how he had got the extra information. He had to pass himself off as more visionary than the rest of the biologists rather than more adventurous and more unscrupulous. In a rush to back him, sponsors in big business did not ask Patrick too many questions. And Patrick used their money to buy the plot of land that became the Finch Private Fertility Clinic.

He believed that success justified what he had done, and whatever experiments he would do in the future, but he still couldn't easily get to sleep. At one time or another, he and his clinic, his methods and aims, had been called evil, grotesque, deplorable, shameful, repulsive and execrable. All manner of substances had been pushed through his door: animal dung, petrol, human excrement, blood, every conceivable type of junk. The sticks and stones that came regularly through his windows stung him but those words hurt even more. They also made him more stubborn. His obsession with being the first person to clone a whole human being remained intact. He still believed that sexuality, mating rituals, the biological attraction of males and females, and the chance coming together of sperm and egg were things of the past. In Patrick's future, children would be the products of careful and proper design. In Patrick's imagined future, clones would be better, healthier people.

By one o'clock, Patrick's restless doze finally became something deeper. He didn't hear his son pattering lightly down the stairs and keying his code into the security system so he could get away without setting off the alarm.

The van lurched round a corner, its wheels against the grass verge. Jordan looked askance at Maynard. "Are you sure you know what you're doing?"

"Tadpole gave me a driving lesson. And I memorized a map. I'm very quick to learn." Maynard had borrowed the SPACE Buggy. Now, he was speeding towards Fairway Pharmaceuticals.

Still dubious, Jordan asked, "Did this Tadpole tell you about driving licences, tax, passing a test, and stuff like that?"

"It's for one night only. It wasn't worth going through all the formalities."

Jordan shook his head. He was being driven by a boy who'd never been in a van before and who hadn't got a licence. In the back, there was an illegal immigrant and a collection of tools for breaking and entering. They had brought Lights Out for dealing with any resistance and SPACE's wire cutters, crowbars, master keys, glass cutters, hammers and everything else for getting into Fairway Pharmaceuticals. "We're not so much breaking the law as slaughtering it and jumping up and down on its dead body." Jordan just had to hope they wouldn't be stopped. Quietly, so that Lights Out in the back of the noisy van could not hear, Jordan added, "You're from the future. You should be able to beam us in."

"Pardon?"

"That device you mentioned – a transporter. Pull the lever and we're beamed wherever we want to go. Just like that. Result."

"Oh." Maynard looked embarrassed. "Er . . . no. It wouldn't do for this sort of thing. Anyway, not far now."

"I've been thinking about the future," Jordan said, still keeping his voice down. "What about film stars, royalty or geniuses? Don't their fans try to get their DNA so they can make clones to have as their own kids?"

"We don't have royalty and anyone can buy genius genes, but celebrities won't kiss, lick, shake hands or do anything that might leave a cell behind. If they buy a drink, they buy the glass as well and take it away to stop anyone getting a DNA sample off it. They're scared stiff someone will clone them." Maynard shrugged as if he didn't understand the fuss.

"Weird. And what's this about the weather?"

"The planet's full of extremes. Two-thirds of Bangladesh is under water. The floods, starvation and disease took six million lives." Still keeping his eyes on the road, Maynard shook his head sadly. "Mozambique's uninhabitable because of floods but other parts of Africa have permanent droughts and famines. Australia and Brazil are almost always on fire. Do you know the Maldives, Tuvalu, Kiribati and islands like that?"

"I think I've seen them in holiday brochures."

"Not in my day. They're submerged under rising sea levels. Florida's under water as well and California's been destroyed by mudslides. The sea's having a good go at reclaiming much of the Netherlands. As for here, it got warmer up to 2100 but then the Gulf Stream broke down and a mini ice age started. Westford's freezing. Literally."

"Bloody hell!"

Maynard slowed, turned left, switched off the van lights and crawled quietly up an unlit lane to Fairway Pharmaceuticals.

Amazed, Jordan turned in his seat. "How are you doing this without crashing?"

"I can see quite well in the dark."

Screwing up his eyes, Jordan couldn't make out anything beyond the windscreen. "Come on! There's more to it than eating carrots."

"Carrots?"

"They're supposed to help you see in the dark."

"Really? I've got the modern equivalent. I'm fitted with a range of sensory improvements: heightened vision, sense of smell and awareness of direction."

"It's all in the genes, eh?"

"A cat's night vision, a dog's sense of smell and a bird's sense of direction."

Maynard pulled up outside a small isolated factory, little more than a large bungalow.

"So, you're part animal."

"No. When you eat beef you don't become part cow."

"That's different," Jordan objected.

"Maybe, but you take up the cow's molecules. Anyway. . ." Maynard left the key in the ignition in case they had to make a quick getaway. "Come on. Let's get in there."

Outside, Jordan could see the squat building a little better. "It's not exactly a multinational." The place was screened on one side by trees and there was a reservoir on the other. A wavering moon floated on the water, stirred gently by the breeze. The only other buildings that they could see lay reassuringly in the distance. Given what he was about to do, Jordan felt comforted by the separation of the laboratory from the rest of the world.

"It's a start-up company, a family business, but it's destined for great things."

Jordan whispered, "It'd be easy to burn down."

"That would slow them up. But they think they've got a huge product. They won't give up on it. They'll begin again."

"At least the place won't be overflowing with high security and guards," said Jordan.

132

They went to the back of the van to get the tools and to release Lights Out from his metal cage. "Come on," Jordan said. "Leave your sandwich toaster here. It'll be safe."

The iron gates were padlocked but there was no sign of video surveillance or wires that would suggest an alarm. Maynard forced a small jemmy into the lock, bent it back and snapped the shackle. "We're in."

"*Karosho*," Lights Out muttered, as if he knew what was going on.

While Jordan looked around to make sure a police squad wasn't closing in on them, Maynard untangled the chain and opened the gate. The three of them slipped inside and walked softly to the entrance, the tools in the holdall making the occasional clanking noise.

The front door was protected by a sturdy metal shutter. Getting through it wasn't impossible with SPACE's tools but it would be difficult and time-consuming. Instead, they went round the side of the brick building and found a window. A shutter was pulled down over it but this one was secured only by another padlock. The crowbar soon shattered it. They pushed up the metal shutter to reveal the glass.

"Can you see in?" Jordan asked. To him, the window was a black hole.

"It's a small lab," answered Maynard. "No obvious security measures."

Surprised, Lights Out said, "Good *glassa*." Pointing to his own face, he translated, "Eyes."

"I'll do the window," Jordan said. He reached into the holdall and extracted a plunger. He licked his fingers and then wetted the rubber rim with them. Then, he pushed the plunger against the window pane until suction held it firmly in place. Using a diamond cutter, he made a deep scratch in the glass all around the plunger. Then he said to the other two, "I read about this on the Internet. How to break glass without making a sound. Here we go." He held the end of the plunger in one hand and smacked it with the other.

The glass broke but did not crash to the floor and smash. The round piece that Jordan had knocked out was still attached to the plunger. Carefully, he pulled it back through the gap, leaving a porthole.

Maynard congratulated him. "Good trick."

"Lights Out, can you reach in and open the window?"

"*Karosho.*"

The window swung open and, one after the other, they clambered into the room. Before Jordan levered himself upwards and through the open window, he handed the holdall to Maynard, already inside. All the time, Jordan was steeling himself for the sudden sound of an alarm but there was nothing.

They were in a still, enclosed laboratory. There were glowing pinpoints of amber from unidentifiable machines on standby but no movement or sound. In one corner, a device displayed the time: 02:17. The intruders did not dare to turn on the lab light or use a torch from the holdall in case they were spotted.

To Maynard, the room held the faint and sickly smell of death. It was a place where sacrificed animals were examined, where their skin was assessed for extent of tanning, damage and cancer. He decided not to tell the others. Leading them, he walked unerringly round the central bench, with its scalpels and microscopes, to the door. Jordan could not even see the door until he was through it and looking into a short dark corridor like a cave.

Maynard paused, pricking up his ears.

Behind him, Jordan whispered, "What?"

"A scrabbling noise. Laboratory animals, I think. Probably rats or mice," Maynard replied.

Jordan tried to settle his nerves by a casual joke. "Do you have an owl's ears as well?" he said quietly so that Lights Out could not hear. His voice cracked with tension.

"No. Good hearing's inbred," Maynard replied, taking the question seriously. "This way." He set out down the corridor.

Jordan suspected that the cat in Maynard had seen a door to the animal laboratory. Maybe the dog in him had smelled the animals and was guiding him faithfully to the right place. At least when they'd done what they had to do, the trusty homing pigeon in Maynard would not fail to get them out again. Being with Maynard made Jordan feel less vulnerable. He also suspected that Maynard's highly developed hearing would easily be able to detect his thudding heart, like a bat tuning in to a nervous fluttering insect.

Lights Out tagged along behind with a smile, showing no sign of stress. For him, the shadowy building was an adventure playground. The law probably didn't figure in his limited vocabulary.

It was so dark, Jordan might as well have shut his eyes. He followed immediately behind Maynard, listening to his footfalls. Luckily, the passageway was absolutely straight. They reached the end and came to a halt. Lights Out bumped into Jordan. Maynard put out his hand, turned the door handle and then it happened.

A high-pitched siren hammered on their skulls. It was incredibly, unbearably loud. Jordan and Maynard were frozen to the spot, bent over in agony, clutching the sides of their heads. Every brain cell between Jordan's ears seemed to go into violent vibration, giving him an instant searing headache. The sound of their cries was swallowed completely by the relentless unearthly wail.

16

Maynard's fine hearing was being assaulted from all sides. But he could not give in to the piercing din. Keeping his palms clamped over his ears, desperate to function despite the torment, he looked up and scoured the walls and ceiling with his enhanced eyes. Spotting the inconspicuous loudspeaker, he took one hand away from the side of his head, grabbed Lights Out's arm and used it to point briefly up at the speaker.

Lights Out was also troubled by the siren. He was frowning with the pain but he had not been disabled by it. His partial deafness, inherited from his grandfather, saved him from the worst effects. Understanding Maynard at once, he reached up on tiptoe and, using his giant's reach, groped around the ceiling until his fingers felt the hidden speaker. Stretching, he just managed to grasp it in one hand and rip it away from its fixing. At once the clamour stopped, leaving an utter vacuum.

After a few seconds, Jordan and Maynard both uttered quiet groans that were snatched away by the dreadful silence. Their heads throbbed, their ears still rang and they felt hopelessly sick as if the noise had loosened the contents of their guts. Both boys swallowed over and over again to bring back feeling to their ears and to keep the vomit down.

"*Gromkey*," Lights Out muttered, grimacing.

Guessing what he'd said, Maynard replied, "*Very* loud."

Jordan could barely hear the other two. Their words seemed to be filtered through an overpowering buzz. "That wasn't a normal alarm. No one has an alarm like that."

"No," Maynard replied. "I think it wasn't designed to alert someone to a break-in. It was to incapacitate intruders. An acoustic weapon – a very effective device. Except that. . ." He glanced at Lights Out and smiled. Without his friend's abnormal height and his deafness, Maynard and Jordan would both have been put out of action, their ears damaged permanently, their bodies in trauma, probably unconscious. In the dark, Maynard's nod of appreciation went unseen. "Let's hope no one heard," he added.

"It was enough to wake the dead," Jordan said, trying to make the best out of a diabolical situation and a dreadful feeling of nausea. "We're about to be caught red-handed by zombies."

"We'd better get on with it, then." Maynard turned round and entered the second laboratory.

It was a small animal house, lit here and there like a nightclub with blue and ultraviolet spotlights. It had no exterior windows at all so it was safe for Maynard to turn on the main lights. The other two boys appeared, blinking, in the doorway.

Down both sides of the room, there were rows of numbered cages containing rats, mice and rabbits like battery farm animals. They had been making scratching noises but now they were motionless, crouching, still stunned and terrified by the shrill siren. Jordan knew exactly how miserable they felt. Most of them had patches of skin that had been shaved bare. Some had bald patches on their backs, some on their legs, fronts, faces, necks. The exposed pieces of skin displayed every conceivable tint. Some were a normal grey colour, others were bright red through extreme sunburn, others were well tanned and dark. In the centre of the lab, several live animals had been pinned down in metal cages with their shaved areas exposed to harsh sun-lamps.

The room was packed with sunbathers, like a crowded holiday resort. Some were crammed into cheap hotel rooms while others claimed positions on the beach. Soon, tomorrow probably, they would be shuffled round. Some would nurse their sunburn in the shade, others would take their places under the ultraviolet lamps. In this place, though, sunbathing was enforced and not enjoyed.

The sight distracted Jordan from his unsettled stomach and splitting head.

"The company's doing what you'd expect," Maynard announced. "Testing the animals' reaction to intense UV light with and without sunscreen."

"Nasty." Jordan took his digital camera from his pocket and snapped a few of the cruellest sights. But he wasn't convinced that splashing yet more torture across the front pages would provoke riots on the street. It would certainly stir up the animal rights activists but the rest of the population might merely see a drug company battling the curse of cancer, protecting human beings, at the expense of a few pests. Jordan and Maynard needed a different tactic to discredit the company and destroy all confidence in its sunblock.

Maynard sat down at the computer and began to delve into the toxicity files. He typed at speed, planting dire results and inserting notes about the need to check the sperm counts of male animals. His annotations warned that the offending sunscreen would not pass the required safety standards if it affected fertility.

When Jordan and Maynard looked round, they saw that Lights Out had released a couple of sunburnt rats and was cradling the frightened, docile creatures in his hands.

"No wonder Myleene likes you," Jordan said. "The gentle giant thing gets her every time."

"It's a good idea, though," Maynard added.

"What is?" asked Jordan.

"We take a few of them. The ones with the least sunburn. They'll be the ones who've been covered with the sunblock."

Jordan had been shaken first by the siren. Now he was shaken by Maynard's scheming. "You want me to get them tested at the clinic!"

Speaking up, Maynard said to Lights Out, "Just make sure they're male."

"Male?" Lights Out queried.

"Boy rats, boy mice, boy rabbits."

"*Kak?*"

Maynard smiled. "If you're asking how you know the difference, it's the usual way."

"I'll help." Recovering his sense of humour, Jordan said, "It's easy. The boys fight and the girls talk about each other behind their backs."

Maynard turned his attention to the computer again.

"Wait. It's even easier. I can tell from these files how many times they've had the sunscreen applied. We want male ones that've had lots of exposure. OK. Grab rabbit S1034 and K0042, rats R0118 and R0756, and a mouse. D0209 will do. The numbers are on the cages." He repeated the code numbers while Jordan searched for the animals like a guard plucking lucky prisoners from death row.

When they'd gathered the five specimens, Maynard typed: *We have taken male animals that have had long-term treatment with your sunscreen. We will test their sperm counts and publicize the results if you do not check it out. When you discover there is a serious side-effect, we expect you to abandon the project. We also have photographs of this lab and the animal experiments. We would have no need to destroy Fairway's reputation if you developed a different formula that is not an endocrine disrupter.*

Reading over Maynard's shoulder, Jordan commented, "Very polite again."

"Let's get out."

"Good idea." Delicately, Jordan bent down to pick up his caged rat and the SPACE holdall. When he stood upright, he felt dizzy and he had to wait for a few seconds to steady himself. The other two grabbed a couple of cages each. "OK. I'm right behind you," Jordan said.

With the hostages stowed safely in the back of the van, Lights Out played the part of zookeeper. In the front, Jordan tried hard to relieve his nervous tension by chattering nonsense. "You know," he said, "whether we like an animal or not depends on how many legs it's got."

"Does it?" Maynard asked, surprised.

"Sure. Two legs, good. Four legs, very good. No legs, bad. More than four legs, very bad indeed. Do you know anyone who likes snakes or spiders?"

"What about dolphins? No legs but loved. And rats. Four legs but hated."

"I didn't say the rule was perfect – and it only applies to animals that live on dry land really. But dolphins and rats come under another rule: the size rule. Basically, the bigger a creature is, like a dolphin or a horse, the nicer. Once you're smaller than a cat, you're generally in trouble, even if you've got four legs. Small and no legs spells complete disaster. Witness the slimy slug."

"If people object to doing experiments on cats, they should object to using rats as well. It's not just the nice fluffy ones that have rights, if you believe in animal rights. Anyway, we've got what we need." Maynard jerked his aching head towards the back.

Jordan sighed. "You want me to tell Dad what we've done, don't you? He'll murder me!"

"Well, tell him exactly *why* we've done it then."

"And that'll make him happy?"

Driving amateurishly, Maynard glanced briefly at his companion. "Yes. Your father really *cares* about fertility. You know he does."

"Too much."

"We've got to delay wrecking his cloning programme, delay the blackmail, and we can recruit him to the cause. If you tell him something's a threat to male fertility, he'll do what we want because he cares. Genuinely."

Jordan grunted. "That doesn't mean he'll give me a round of applause for breaking and entering."

"OK. Don't let on that you were involved. Tell him an activist who's concerned about a new sunscreen gave you the animals. Then he'll agree to test them. And if he finds they're sterile, he'll make a big fuss as well. He'll be angry."

"This is some turnaround, planning to make my dad a hero."

Not concentrating hard enough on driving, Maynard switched on the wipers when he meant to indicate left. "Right now, I'd recruit the devil himself if I thought it'd save the world."

Anti Clone was livid with Space Cadet. "You – you and Jordan Finch – have decided to put direct action on hold! Well, so much for SPACE being democratic. You're not going to have a go at the clinic with the photos you say you've got. Instead you're working some mysterious plot with some nicked lab animals. And you say we've just got to trust you. But you've given them to Finch as well. Do they exist any more than the pictures? If they do, you're giving up all our best weapons. Pathetic." Exasperated, she shook her head and added, "I'm not going to let you ruin everything we've been working towards for so long." Not waiting for Maynard to respond, she stormed away in a grand gesture of frustration and defiance.

Gaia Queen, eager to dismiss the tantrum, looked closely at Lights Out. He was wearing his usual threadbare jacket but its right pocket now seemed to have a will of its own. "Lights Out, why does your pocket keep moving?"

Finally free of his headache, Maynard glanced at his friend and down at his wriggling jacket pocket. "Did you smuggle another mouse out?"

Lights Out grinned and extracted a restless rat from his pocket.

Gaia Queen let out an appreciative sigh. "Ahh. Poor thing."

"It's a rat, not a mouse," Maynard said in a raised voice. "Why did you keep it?"

Lights Out looked pleased with himself. "For Myleene."

Maynard nodded. "She gives you a sandwich toaster that you can't use and you give her a rat."

"Da."

"It won't make much of a fur coat."

"Space Cadet!" exclaimed Gaia Queen.

"Not seriously," Maynard responded. He reached up and put a hand on Lights Out's shoulder. "I'm not very good at this sort of thing but, you know, I'm not convinced that Myleene will appreciate a rat. Especially one that's had it's backside shaved."

All three of them looked round as the SPACE Buggy revved alarmingly. With Anti Clone at the wheel, it made for the locked metal gates of the fertility clinic. Instead of slowing, it accelerated. On the other side of the barrier, guards scattered in all directions.

Realizing immediately what Anti Clone had in mind, Maynard stood open-mouthed in horror.

Metal met metal in a thunderous crash. The padlocked gates buckled inwards under the impact but held together. The van's bonnet crumpled as the vehicle shuddered to a halt and the engine tangled with the brutal upright supports. There was an awful wrenching sound as the front of the van merged with the gates, becoming an indistinguishable mass of twisted steel.

The startled rat leapt from Lights Out's limp inattentive hand. In a second grand gesture, Anti Clone was catapulted through the van's windscreen on to the unforgiving bars and sturdy spikes.

17

The lamb lay on the table, outwardly like any other lamb, and much improved since that first illicit experiment with Sarah, but dead all the same. As soon as it had been born, some time in the night, it had suffered breathing difficulties. It had gasped continually, pathetically, as if exhausted by a gruelling birth. Now, Kayleigh invited Patrick to look through the microscope at a blood vessel from the lamb's lung tissue. The almost colourless cavity was massive, twenty times larger than a normal lamb's. "Its heart couldn't pump blood properly through blood vessels that size," Kayleigh said. "The poor thing didn't stand a chance. Nowhere near enough oxygen. That's why it panted like a dog on a hot day. I'm logging it as having the same circulatory abnormalities as we've seen before."

Patrick nodded solemnly. He was consoled, though, by the thought that if this specimen had been human rather than ovine, it would not have got to the point of being born. A dead baby, externally disfigured or internally inadequate, would be much worse than no baby at all. His screening method would detect enlarged blood vessels in a tiny foetus, maybe even at the embryo stage. Then he would abort the pregnancy like a launch supervisor abandoning a lift-off as soon as he detected a fault in a rocket booster.

Back in his office, his computer bleeped him. Patrick

was pleased to see that Churchman had merely added an insult to their long-running dispute.

Churchman: *I return to the issue of the defective embryos you throw out callously. This is a sin and you are a murderer. An embryo is a developing human being with the same moral standing as a child. It has got to have the same rights and protection as any other human being. It is not a research commodity and it cannot be discarded willy-nilly.*

Patrick: *Natural pregnancies kill embryos. For every naturally conceived embryo that develops into a baby, there will be about five that get discarded willy-nilly by nature. You wouldn't accuse every mother of murder so don't accuse me either.*

Churchman: *You plan murder cold-bloodedly. You do it on purpose.*

Patrick: *An embryo is a blob of cells smaller than a pinhead, with not even the faintest hint of human-ness. It is like the clumps of cells we wash off our skin and flush down the plughole every day. It does not deserve rights.*

Churchman: *There is a world of difference between an embryo and a bit of dandruff.*

Patrick: *I can make a bit of dandruff into a child. In theory, each and every living cell in your body could be cloned and made into an embryo with the potential to be a human being. Is every flake of skin, every drop of blood, every hair follicle sacred? Of course not. Otherwise, you would commit murder every time you scratch an itch and kill off thousands of skin cells.*

Churchman: *Let's have an intelligent exchange. As I understand it, the biological identity, appearance and temperament* of a clone would be determined, like any other child, straight after you fertilize the egg. Fertilization is the start of human life so an embryo is not a disposable ball of cells, it is a budding human being.

Patrick: *That is an irrelevant emotional argument, not scientifically correct. There is no sex act in cloning. New life comes into being without conception and without fertilization. How can you define the start of human life as fertilization of the woman's egg when I can make life without it?*

Churchman: *You miss my point. That is exactly why you should not be cloning. You are making new life but not true life, not a new combination of genes. Everyone born has a right to be unique.*

Patrick: *Nonsense. Nature has been making identical twins – with identical genes – for centuries. It is no big deal. You do not need a man in a white coat to do that.*

Churchman: *Just because nature makes the same slip sometimes, that does not give you licence to manufacture identical twins on purpose. Your men in white coats are tampering with nature.*

Patrick: *Actually, cloning is not unnatural. Bacteria, yeasts and your common or garden aphid reproduce by cloning. The aphid only uses sex every few generations. Artemia shrimps have survived for 30-odd million years by cloning themselves.*

Churchman: *You are well-read but all that is beside the point. Cloning is not natural for human beings. Your arrogance puts us on a slippery slope.*

Patrick: *You mean, like we tampered with nature to get rid of polio and smallpox, and to save millions with penicillin?*

148

That slippery slope led to a better, healthier world. Even if you do regard an embryo as alive, you are still wrong. It is not life as such that we value, or we would not eat living plants and we would not swat flies, step on spiders or put poison down for ants. It is feelings we value. We eat fruit and kill cockroaches because they do not have feelings. Embryos do not have feelings either. They cannot have feelings because they have not grown a nervous system.

And then came the name-calling.

Churchman: *It is morally reprehensible, unnatural and repugnant, and you are unscrupulous.*

Patrick was pleased because he knew that he was winning an argument when his adversary resorted to abuse.

Patrick: *There was a similar outcry about "test-tube babies" in the 1970s, especially from the church and the media. Terrible, horrible. But it quickly blew over. Today IVF treatments are not controversial. They are a real boon to the ten per cent of married couples who are infertile. But it took ages to be accepted, about a decade. Cloning is no different. It is another cure that upsets the church and the media but, when it starts producing babies who could not otherwise be born, people will come to understand it, see the benefits and think of it as normal. The heat will die down and it will be incorporated into the arsenal of fertility treatments. The yuk factor will disappear eventually.*

149

He sat back for a moment and turned his mind to the serious issues. When it came to cloning human beings, he would take a few cells from every growing embryo for testing and freeze any viable ones with the desired genetic make-up and no abnormalities, ready for implantation into the woman's womb at the right time. He thought again about Churchman's objections and reached for the phone. To his colleague in Barbados, he said, "All human embryos that don't pass the genetic screening, we're going to put them into deep freeze."

"Why? That's a waste of time, money and space. The abnormal ones are no use."

"We can store billions in one small liquid nitrogen tank. That's no great drain on us."

"Why do it, though?"

Patrick replied, "If we freeze them for ever we can truthfully say we don't cull potential human beings. Instead we're keeping them in cryopreservation until we learn how to fix their genetic hiccups."

"We'll never do that."

"No," Patrick agreed. "But that's irrelevant."

"Ah. I see. Why didn't you say so? You're talking politics, not biology."

"Exactly. But we have to get both right. We have to avoid the embarrassment of being accused of 'killing' embryos."

"Well, politically speaking, that'd do it."

Patrick's face was a mixture of disbelief and dismay. "Let me get this right," he said to Jordan as if he were talking to a young child. "You know some animal rights people and, in the middle of last night, they brought these lab animals round in a van. Rabbits and rodents. And you've put them in your room!"

"Yes. But—"

"And that's why your mum tells me we didn't have security switched on twice last night?"

"But you haven't heard why—" Jordan tried to say.

"Was that the same van some girl slammed into the gate at work today and got herself impaled on the railings?"

Jordan's eyes opened wide. "What? Really? That's horrible. But I don't know. There's a lot of vans in the world. And a lot of protesters."

"Well, this one thought she was a lemming."

"You mean, she did it on purpose? She wasn't just trying to crash into the grounds?"

"We don't know," Patrick replied. "Either way, she was stupid."

Jordan saw contempt rather than compassion in his father. If Jordan showed much sympathy for the girl, if he praised her self-sacrificing dedication, his dad would regard him as a traitor. He couldn't afford to make an enemy of his father right now. He had to keep to the point. "Anyway, I only said I'd have these animals because I think you'll be interested in them."

Interrupting again, Patrick asked, "Interested? Why would I be interested in stolen animals?"

Jordan had dosed himself with paracetamol. He needed it for his head and he needed it to get through this. It felt like a very unfriendly interview. "Because you care about fertility," he answered.

"They're not intersex animals, are they?"

"What?" Jordan said. "I'm talking about falling sperm counts."

"Again? Tell me what's going on, then." Patrick sat down as if he were in for a long haul.

At least he didn't keep butting in while Jordan spun a yarn about a group of environmentalists that had liberated the creatures from Fairway Pharmaceuticals over fears about endocrine disrupters.

As he listened, Patrick became less concerned with his son's foolishness and more drawn into the intrigue. After all, his was a fight for the right of men, of couples, to have children. He didn't want to knock down barriers in his clinic only to have some inexperienced drug company erect different ones. "How did you get involved?" he asked Jordan.

"Oh, one of the group's at school and he knew what you worked on. He thought you'd help."

Patrick pondered on it for a moment. "What you say makes sense. After a pesticide got spilled in a lake in Florida, turtles that should have been male were neither male nor female. They were in-between."

It was Jordan's turn to interrupt. "Is that what you meant by intersex?"

"Yes. Courtesy of an endocrine disrupter in the pollution, they were nowhere near being viable fathers. Complete loss of sperm. Male fish near sewage outlets in Britain have been known to turn female as well, though no one knows exactly what's causing it. Possibly the chemicals that keep plastics from going brittle. Anyway, it doesn't

152

bode well for men. A while back, I read a paper on a crack-pot idea that, at least in theory, some new suntan lotion could be an endocrine disrupter."

"Maybe not so crackpot." It made a pleasant change for Jordan to find himself on the same wavelength as his dad. He smiled. "So, you'll test the animals at work?"

"I'm not condoning your mates breaking the law but, now they have, I might as well try and extract some good from it. I can't do a proper study, not without the animals' full records, the suntan lotion, and a lot more experiments, but I can soon assess their reproductive health. I'll get it done before I go off to the Caribbean."

"Thanks, Dad."

"They did take male animals, didn't they?" Patrick had low expectations of all activists.

"Of course."

"Just checking."

Jordan decided to make the most of this friendly man-to-man chat. He tried not to hesitate, not to seem anxious, as he asked, "Was she on her own, the girl who was killed at the clinic?"

"Luckily, it was a solo performance."

Jordan nodded and struggled to avoid appearing too relieved.

18

In the dead of the night, both Patrick and Gwen lay awake. Quietly, Gwen said, "You're never going to convert him to your way of thinking, you know."

"No, I don't suppose so," Patrick muttered. "Nor you."

"I've tried but. . ."

"No, I meant I'm not going to convert you either," Patrick replied.

Shocked, Gwen sat up in the dark. "Me? I've always supported you. Always."

"Yes. I know. And I'm grateful. But help and support isn't the same as approval."

"I've always approved of your intentions – working miracles for the childless."

Patrick's body rocked with quiet ironic laughter. "I'm not sure the church would class my work among the great miracles."

"I do, though."

"You believe in my aims, not my methods."

Gwen hesitated before replying, "I wish there was another way, that's all. There isn't, so. . . But Jordan doesn't see it like that. If you do this animal work for him, take an interest in his stuff, it'd be great but you won't get him on your side."

"I know. I'll test his animals because it's the right thing

to do. Though, tonight's the first time in a long time a chat with Jordan hasn't left a bad taste. It was . . . wonderful actually. Reminded me of years ago, before the rebellious teenager stage."

Gwen smiled. "No one can go back in time." She lay down again and said, "You know, he started acting strange after he found that activist in the back garden."

"Now you mention it, yes. I wonder. . ." Patrick never reached the end of the sentence.

"What?"

"Nothing," Patrick muttered.

Myleene and Anita had promised their parents that they'd settle down straight after getting back from the nightclub. Of course, they didn't. Myleene sat on Neat's bed and they talked in hushed voices well into the early hours.

"Myleene?"

"Mmm?"

"What's bothering you?" asked Neat.

"Nothing."

"Since when have we been able to hide anything from each other?"

"All right," Myleene replied. "It's Lights Out."

Neat cocked her head. "Oh?"

"Since when have I had to tell you what I'm thinking?" said Myleene, getting her own back.

Anita nodded. "You really like him. And it bothers you that I do as well."

"You should be concentrating on Tim."

"Tim's all right, I suppose, but. . ." Anita shrugged.

"How come we both fall for a guy who can hardly speak the language?"

"*Because* he can hardly speak the language." Myleene managed a wry grin. "Once most boys open their mouths, it's . . . you know." She grimaced.

"A big disappointment."

"To put it mildly."

"And he's pretty deaf as well."

"Perfect," Myleene replied with a giggle. "You can nag him all day and he'll just smile sweetly."

Anita nodded. "OK. He's cute, but I blame our hormones. We're just trying to get on with life, doing sensible things, when they take over and lead us into all sorts of trouble."

Suddenly serious again, Myleene asked, "What are we going to do?"

With a bright red face, Jordan stared at the watch. It was never going to work again. He was convinced. All the king's horses and all the king's men were not going to put this one back together again. Not even Maynard, he suspected. It would need a specialist watchmaker – one that wasn't even born yet. So, Jordan was torn. Being too late to salvage the watch, he could carry on studying its power source and not say a word to Maynard. Or he could risk Maynard's reaction and confess what he had done. Jordan knew which was the right thing to do. He also knew what he wanted to do.

Just like his dad had done before him, Jordan continued his secretive and destructive investigation of the innards.

He too was keen to learn by performing an intricate and thorough post-mortem.

A gulf had opened up in SPACE City since the campaign had claimed its first martyr. The more militant members redoubled their protest. In balaclavas, they were twice as rowdy at the gates of the clinic, twice as imaginative when it came to making nuisances of themselves. The rest of the camp was muted. Yet no one was thinking of giving up – that would have infuriated Anti Clone. There was anger, there was sadness, there was determination, but all of the fun had gone out of it.

Troubled, Maynard peeped out from the door of his tent at the unfamiliar wild daffodils. They were well past their best but they still looked wonderful to him. Yet they did not distract him for long. He was occupied more with Anti Clone's sacrifice. She had killed herself for her cause and that single-mindedness frightened Maynard. He also felt admiration – and shame because, in a way, he was responsible. Anti Clone was dispirited with the lack of progress. For her, removing the need for cloning was not enough. She was trying for a spectacular stepping up of the action against the process itself. And really she was right. In this world there were tens of millions of men who could not be fathers but, even if there had been just ten, Patrick Finch would still have come to their aid. The power to clone humans was almost within his grasp. He was like a heron with a large eel writhing in its beak, not quite in control of the slippery thing, but determined not to let go of a tasty meal.

If Jordan's ploy to seed the destruction of endocrine disrupters worked, if Patrick Finch played a key part in that campaign, the whole game plan would have to shift. How could Maynard and Jordan enlist Patrick's help over the sunscreen issue and, at the same time, disgrace him over reproductive cloning? Anti Clone would not have approved of a hands-off-Finch mode. Or perhaps she saw it coming and the crash was her rage against it.

Even at dawn, SPACE City swarmed with journalists, cameras, microphones and police officers. A police ribbon cordoned off the gates and the smashed van until the forensic scientists had collected every scrap of information from the scene. Maynard and Lights Out stayed in their tent because they had no wish to be interviewed either by the police or by reporters.

The Finch Private Fertility Clinic was quiet on a Saturday morning. But Patrick was in work, instructing a technician to carry out sperm tests on Jordan's animals. "And," he added, "while you're doing that, there's something else. It's just a hunch. . . Anyway, I need an urgent DNA profile on a sperm sample. It's from a lad who I'm pretty sure came in with my son on Wednesday. I can't remember his name. Anyway, dig it out and do the analysis for me, will you? I want to compare it with forensic files."

Patrick became even more eager to test his wild theory about Jordan's friend when the police reported that they had discovered Jordan's fingerprints on the inside of the wrecked van. The police kept the Finch family's prints on record in case they ever had to investigate a break-in at their house. To identify any fingerprints belonging to intruders, they would first need to eliminate those from Patrick, Gwen and Jordan.

Of course, the police finding was not necessarily evidence of any treachery by Jordan. He could have been in the van merely to collect those hijacked animals. No doubt that's what Jordan would claim if Patrick were to confront him. But even so, Patrick felt an ominous heaviness in his stomach.

At least the sperm counts on Fairway's animals diverted him. None of them was up to scratch sexually and two were pathetic so it seemed that Jordan and his friends were right. Immediately Patrick logged on to the scientific literature and drew up a shopping list of chemicals regarded as possible gender-benders. Then he called in a colleague and asked her to buy the substances, design a proper study and stock the laboratory with the animals that she would need. "This is going to be high profile," Patrick announced heatedly. "When we get watertight evidence against any of these, we publish far and wide. It'll destroy the companies that make them. And we're starting with Fairway's new sunblock."

"I can see why you'd want to. . ."

"You should be able to see why any human – the world – would want me to do it."

"Yes," she agreed. "And it'll put the clinic in a good light for a change. You'll get some welcome publicity. But where's the money coming from?"

"Rich oil tycoons who think their manhood's suffering will cough up. If not, I'll fund it from cloning profits. It's worth it."

The fight for the future of male fertility had begun.

The identical twin with an identical present slipped into SPACE City, hoping not to be noticed by security guards, cameras, and especially not by the police. Once a protester had pointed out the tent where Lights Out was laying low, Anita hurried towards it. Under her arm she had a box containing a sandwich toaster.

19

Despite the tense atmosphere at home, Jordan was buoyant. "Dad's got his teeth into his new project. He's set up a special unit to look into endocrine disrupters properly. That's a result. So now's a good time."

"What?" Maynard exclaimed. "We can't set the press on him if he's on our side."

"I'm not talking about that, not sending the monkey photos to the newspapers. Not any more," Jordan said. "Remember my plan? You write – we write – that letter, telling Dad to stop cloning *or else* the chimpanzee goes to the press. He wouldn't want to risk that. It's called blackmail."

Even sitting at the rear of the café, Jordan and Maynard could hear tuneless voices singing a crude song in the road at the front. Police officers on horses, foot patrols and their dogs were herding the rowdy but good-natured fans towards the football stadium. Out of the window, the boys could see the incessant stream of supporters surging diagonally across the park and shuffling through the turnstile like grains of sand dribbling through an hourglass. "If it's left to Dad," Jordan said, watching the fans, "football managers'll clone their best players. You'll hear crowds chanting, 'There's only eleven Michael Owens.' That'd be another result."

Maynard didn't understand the joke. Solemnly, he

announced, "Blackmail won't work. Your dad'll just go abroad and do it there."

"It's worth a try, I say. Maybe he'll ditch cloning research and stop sperm counts going downhill instead. He'll name the prime suspects – like that new sunscreen. People won't buy it, it won't become a best-seller and, hey, the world's OK again. Even if it doesn't work, I've got another trick up my sleeve."

"A what?"

"Another plan. Something else we could use against Dad but. . ." Jordan hesitated. "I'd rather not."

Maynard sensed that Jordan didn't want to talk about his idea so he didn't ask what it was. Instead, Maynard watched two sparrows tussling outside on the bough of a tree. "It's difficult to say whether they're fighting or mating."

"Yeah," Jordan replied with a smile. "It's like that with humans as well sometimes."

"I still can't get over your weather, the birds and flowers. In my day—"

Jordan interrupted. "You remind me of my grandma. Always going on about the good old days when everything was brilliant. You go on about the bad new days." In an old croaky voice, Jordan said, "'You don't know how lucky you are. In my day, you can skate to France.' Does it mean things just get worse as time goes by?"

Maynard didn't answer but his face told Jordan that life wasn't going to get any easier. "All right," Maynard suddenly replied, "we try your blackmail idea but. . ." He shook his head.

*

Coming home from school on Monday, Jordan caught his mum coming out of his bedroom. Attempting not to look embarrassed, she said, "Oh, hello. Back already? I've just . . . er . . . made your bed up."

Jordan also tried to react normally. "That's a pity. I was hoping for a real one."

Neither of them managed wholehearted grins. Jordan wondered if she had been rummaging through his things so he checked that the chimpanzee folder remained well hidden and undisturbed among his school art projects. He also wondered why his mum might have been going through his bedroom.

By evening, he had the answer. Virtually trembling, he was sitting at the computer, tapping in to the security system. With increasing horror, he was eavesdropping on his parents who thought that they were having a private conversation. Well, if his mum had been snooping on him, he had every right to retaliate.

"But he's your own son!" Gwen cried.

"I know but I can't keep him out of it even if I wanted to."

"Why not?"

Patrick took a breath, clearly trying to keep his patience. "Because he's tied himself to this Litzoff. The DNA sample I've got at the clinic matches the one left on the bush in the back garden. And there's no doubt Jordan got him into work. He stole the photos. Now he's threatening me with them."

"Jordan might not have known. I didn't find anything in his room."

"The police say Jordan and Maynard Litzoff were both in that van."

"That means nothing. Litzoff might be leading him by the nose."

"It's probably only a matter of time before the police prove they were both in Fairways," Patrick replied. "I can't stop the police questioning him, Gwen. He's in too deep. If he's innocent, they'll let him go and he'll have learnt a lesson. If he isn't. . ." He paused. "Nothing I can do."

Jordan hadn't expected it to get this dirty. In breaking into Fairway Pharmaceuticals and plotting against his own father, he was trying to do the world a favour and yet the world was conspiring against him. He felt aggrieved. He also knew that he couldn't wait for the police to come and arrest him – he'd never cope with the questioning. So, under cover of darkness, he slipped out of the house with a few possessions, the chimpanzee file, and all the money he could muster.

At sunset, the dark chimneys at the edge of town looked like cactus plants rising up from a desert. In SPACE City, a man with the unlikely name of Tadpole guessed who Jordan Finch was looking for and directed him to Space Cadet, as Tadpole told Jordan he was called in the camp.

When Jordan undid the flap of the tent, Maynard's face did not show as much shock as Jordan had expected. He didn't even say, "What are you doing here?"

Jordan answered the unasked question anyway. "I've come to warn you. All hell's broken loose at home."

"Oh?"

"Yeah. The police are coming to arrest you. And me.

They've crosschecked your DNA profile with the blood in our garden."

"Ah."

"Is that all you can say? 'Ah.'"

"Well, I'm ready to leave."

Jordan was surprised. "Are you? How come?"

Lights Out pointed to his own ear. "He hears."

Maynard frowned. He didn't want Jordan to know that he had his own eavesdropping method and that he'd been snooping on Jordan's home. Waving a hand towards Lights Out, he said, "He means I'd thought about it and guessed what'd happen. Anyway, I'm always ready for a quick get-away – just in case. I'm not exactly overrun with things that need packing."

Jordan nodded. "I don't know what I'm going to. . ."

Even through the blue nylon, they saw the sweeping headlights. They heard car doors banging shut, the shouts of the police swooping on SPACE City.

"Looks like you only just got here in time," Maynard said at once. "Time to go." He scuttled towards the door, ushering the other two out.

Lights Out hesitated, turning to grab his sandwich toasters.

Maynard allowed himself a brief smile. "Quick! Just one, Lights Out." He held up a finger. "One'll do, surely."

Lights Out nodded. He had to make an instant decision. Myleene's gift or Anita's? He didn't need time. He grabbed Myleene's present and followed Maynard out of the tent.

They kept low, on their knees, peering towards the road where six police cars were creating a blaze of flashing

165

colour. The officers were fanning out across the campsite, their torches creating a shimmering net. They stopped at each tent, dragged out the occupants, and shone spotlights in their faces.

Maynard heard Gaia Queen's scream of indignation and anguish. It was the first time he'd heard her raised voice. "I know who you're looking for," she gasped. "Leave me alone, let me go, and I'll tell you where he is."

There was an inaudible response.

Jordan and Maynard froze, glancing at each other. Silently, Jordan began a countdown to disaster in his head. "Ten and nine and eight and. . ."

"Yes. That's him." It was Gaia Queen's voice again. "He's over there. The big red frame tent."

Both of the boys breathed a sigh of relief and began to crawl away from the clinic entrance and towards the wood behind the camp. There, the tall dark trees offered the promise of refuge. In his mind, Maynard thanked Gaia Queen for buying them a few extra minutes. Most of the police officers dashed towards another part of SPACE City. Lights Out was mystified by the whole business but followed Maynard, copying his movements.

On all fours, they went as quickly as they could. They needed to get right away from the site because, if the police brought in tracker dogs, they would soon be sniffed out and hunted down. Behind them, there were shouts and accusations. The activists who had been removed from the big red tent and lined up outside it were nothing like Maynard Litzoff.

Gaia Queen was acting innocent and bewildered. She

was unnervingly good at it. "Well, he was here earlier. I'm sure he was. Totally."

While Gaia Queen was marched away, a sergeant major's angry voice shouted, "Spread out again and complete the search."

Maynard, Jordan and Lights Out were clear of the last row of tents but the bushes that bound the wood were still a depressing distance away. Without cover, the boys would soon be caught in a spotlight if they stood and made a dash for it. They stayed low. There had not been much rain recently but their palms, elbows and knees became damp and caked with mud. Jordan was praying that the ominous cameras attached to the top of the wall around the clinic were not capable of night vision. Really, though, he guessed that the protesters had smashed them all. Otherwise, the police would have viewed the tapes before the raid to find out which tent was Maynard's.

A policewoman stood at the perimeter of SPACE City and surveyed the no man's land that the boys were crossing clumsily like large and lame lizards. The beam from her torch swung across the field, ever closer to them.

Then there was a yell. "Pigs! You won't get me!" Tadpole took off at high speed back towards the clinic.

The police didn't fall so easily for a second trick. Only three officers bolted after him, thinking he would be Litzoff. Luckily, the policewoman was one of them. She turned off her torch and went in pursuit.

Jordan put his hand on a nettle or a thistle – he couldn't see in the dark – and stifled a cry of pain and shock. Ahead of him, Maynard was wriggling more effectively now, still lizard-like, less lame. He must have amazing upper body strength, Jordan thought, or more genes from a dog than he'd admitted. The muscles in Jordan's arms and shoulders were aching, unaccustomed as he was to crawling like a soldier in enemy territory.

"Not far," Maynard whispered.

He was right. From further back, the wood had a solid silhouette like a huge gloomy painting. Now, Jordan could pick out individual trees. Maynard was leading them to a gap between bushes. Wondering how Lights Out was managing, Jordan glanced round. The lanky boy was lagging behind but he was doing remarkably well considering that he wouldn't let go of his sandwich toaster. Encumbered, he was shuffling along like an ungainly puppy with an over-ambitious plaything. There was no point telling him to drop it, though.

From SPACE City, hostile voices drifted towards them. Police officers were bawling orders, protesters were hurling insults and ridicule.

When Maynard clambered up the small rise and into the wood, he turned and flattened himself to the ground. "Come on," he murmured. Then, more urgently but still quietly, he called, "Stop! Get down!"

A light beam swept across the field and passed right over them, unable to distinguish the inert forms of Jordan and Lights Out from all of the other undulations. Lights Out was protecting his gift with his body. It was just as well, otherwise the torchlight would have picked out the glossy surface of the box.

"OK," Maynard whispered. "Come on again. Hurry!"

Three minutes later, they were huddled together at the edge of the wood, safe for the moment from prying eyes and spotlights.

"We've got to keep moving," Jordan said, rubbing his sore hand. "I dread to think what'd happen if they got dogs on the job. They'd get our smell from inside your tent and they'd be on us in no time. But. . ." He looked into the wood and realized he'd hardly be able to see a step ahead of himself. He pushed his glasses up on to the bridge of his nose.

Picking up Jordan's thoughts, Maynard replied, "It'll be difficult but you can keep close and follow me."

"Oh, yes. You've got cat's eyes, haven't you?"

Maynard said, "If you can't see much, at least no one out there" – he nodded towards the line of police cars – "will be able to see much in here either." And he began to guide them through the dark wood.

"Where are we going?" Jordan asked as he stumbled forward.

"No idea," Maynard answered over his shoulder. "All I know is, we're going north-west and away from being caught."

Jordan no longer had a sense of direction at all. A criminal on the run, he'd broken unexpectedly away from his moorings. He was adrift and scared.

20

The three boys were out of place, not at all where they belonged. They had each made their own choices – one had left his own country, one his own time, and another his own home – but now they had become ensnared in the same unfamiliar land. When Jordan began to challenge his dad's work, he never thought he'd end up on the streets, outlawed, under the grimy railway bridge where Westford's homeless congregated. But that's where Lights Out wanted to go.

To pass the time, to keep his spirits up, Jordan said to Maynard in a quiet voice, "I've been thinking. We'd have got away a lot easier if we'd had wings. Can you add a few more bird genes and give people wings?"

"In theory, yes. The genetic engineering is fairly easy. But why do it? Humans are the wrong shape to fly so it's a waste of time. They'd just look . . . stupid."

"They'd look like angels. That's good. They'd get out of being shepherds in lousy nativity plays. All the little kids want the angel parts."

Maynard replied, "It'd make more sense to give swimmers webbed hands and feet. That'd be useful. They'd swim faster." Abruptly, he sat up, watching Lights Out and a familiar figure.

"What is it?" asked Jordan, also alert. He expected to be surrounded by police at any moment.

Maynard pointed to a squat man in a woolly hat. "I know him."

As Maynard and Jordan approached Lights Out, Manchester United grinned.

"Hey! You still here?" he said. He looked at Jordan and then back at Maynard. "And you're breeding. Now there's two of you that don't look right."

Lights Out was holding his sandwich toaster and a small bunch of papers. "Look," he said to Maynard, holding out the handful of documents.

"What are they?"

Before Lights Out could work out how to explain, Manchester United answered. "Papers. I got 'em. Birth certificate, Brit passport, that sort of thing."

"Really?"

"Forged, like, but class stuff. Nearly the real thing. They're what he needs to get going."

"So," Jordan put in, "what's his official name? He's not called Lights Out in the passport, is he?"

Manchester United shrugged. "I didn't have no name but he sounds, like, Russian. Here's the clever bit." Looking proud of himself, he said, "I changed Lights Out to Lights Off and called 'im Litzoff. Alex Litzoff. Sounds Russian, don't it?"

Jordan was amazed. Open-mouthed, he turned to Maynard. "But that's. . ."

Trying to suppress his own shock, Maynard cut Jordan off straight away. "Er, yeah," he said. "Good name. Very Russian."

Reading Maynard's face, Jordan saw not just astonishment

but realization. Maynard looked like a boy who, after studying a puzzle for years, had just understood how all of the pieces clicked into place. He was also trying hard not to look at Lights Out with a new sense of awe.

When Jordan noticed that Manchester United was staring at him, expecting further congratulations, he said, "A result. Litzoff's more Russian than Lenin, nicer than Ivan the Terrible."

Manchester United looked askance at Jordan, not sure if the new boy had praised him or not.

"Just one thing," Jordan continued. "What's it cost?"

"Cost?"

"Yes. Come on." He waved towards the dodgy documents that Lights Out was grasping. "You don't get that sort of thing for nothing. Not if they're any good."

"They're good all right."

Maynard was hardly listening to the conversation. He had retreated into his own thoughts. Occasionally, though, he glanced at Lights Out.

"So?" Jordan prompted.

"There's nothing to pay. No cash anyway. Lights Out – Alex – just has to do a stint or two on the door of The Slippery Slope now and again. That's the deal. No problem. He'll make a class bouncer."

Maynard became attentive again and nodded as if he'd known the cost all along.

The receipt left with the sandwich toaster in the tent made it easy for the police. They visited the store where it had been purchased on Saturday morning. They scoured the shop's security video tapes until they pinpointed the girl who had bought the toaster with cash. Then they commandeered all of the surveillance footage from nearby banks. The team of officers that trawled through it soon discovered that the same girl had got money from a cash dispenser half an hour before buying the sandwich toaster. Consulting the bank's records gave them her name and address. Simple.

After the police had called to question Anita, Myleene was furious. She was furious because Neat had tried to win over Lights Out with a gift. It was a cynical and sneaky move. Myleene was furious because, now that Lights Out was on the run, she would not see him again.

The sisters' mum was also furious and, for the second time, embarrassed by her wayward daughters' connections to the protest at the fertility clinic. Myleene and Anita were not improving her chances of promotion in the police force. Refusing to allow them to torpedo her career, she grounded them.

Imprisoned together, the girls had ample opportunity to vent their anger, to blame one another, to talk, to quarrel, to expose each other's sensitive spots, to inject venom. Mostly, the time was taken up with arguments and recriminations.

On the way to an inconspicuous hotel, it felt strange not to have Lights Out in tow. At least, Jordan thought, that would make life harder for the police. They were probably searching for three boys, the most distinctive being a young giant. Yet Lights Out had gone off with Manchester United.

Pensive, Maynard seemed to be grieving the loss of his friend.

"You could go to The Slippery Slope tonight," Jordan suggested. "I bet that's where he'll be. They'll probably set him up in a comfy flat as well. He'll be toasting sandwiches till he bursts."

"It's not that," Maynard said.

"What then?" Jordan asked.

"I've got to get Lights Out and Myleene together again. I must."

"Ah, yes. Alex Litzoff and all that. You mean. . ."

Maynard nodded. "It looks like it. Before I came here, they told me I'd do something that'd affect my entire life. I didn't know what they meant but I do now. I think Lights Out is my own ancestor and what I did was introduce him to Myleene. If I mess up, if I don't get them back together, I won't exist."

"That's a creepy thought," Jordan said in a low voice. "But things aren't too bad. I can get Myleene to go to this Slippery Slope club."

"The police'll be watching the twins."

"True. With their mum, the twins have got in-house police surveillance. I'll get Tim to take Anita and Myleene instead."

Maynard looked up, more hopeful. "Yes. OK. That might do it."

"I'll go and see Tim. The police can't be watching every-one. And . . . er. . ."

"What?"

"It's Dad. You said we can't set the hounds on him if he's

on our side. But now he's latched on to endocrine disrupters, he won't let go. He's never been the type to give up. So we *can* have a good go at him over cloning."

"He won't let go of that either."

"Not unless he's forced to."

"What's on your mind?" asked Maynard.

When Jordan still had a bed and a home, he hadn't wanted to use his trump card. He wouldn't have dared. Now everything had changed. "I know something about Dad that would get him thrown out of APART. That's the Association of Private Assisted Reproductive . . . something or other. Anyway, if he gets chucked out, that's it. No licence to operate."

"Yes?"

"Dad got his clinic off the ground because he did an unethical, illegal cloning experiment."

Maynard gazed at Jordan for a few seconds. "I wouldn't know, but isn't it a big thing here to betray your own father?"

Finding an excuse not to answer, Jordan stopped outside a seedy city-centre hotel. "This one'll do. If they had murderers staying here, they still wouldn't inform the police."

"They'll be suspicious."

"But money will talk louder. Are you sure you've. . ."

Maynard pulled a heavy wad of fifty-pound notes from deep within his coat and held it out towards Jordan.

"All right," Jordan muttered. "I wouldn't get it out in public, if I were you. Especially not here." Putting both hands around the cash, he pushed it gently back towards Maynard's pocket.

"It's not a lot of money in my time. Not that it's legal. It's old and worthless. They sent me back with it in case I needed to buy anything."

"You could have been living in luxury with that lot!"

"A tent suited me better. I was more anonymous that way."

Jordan shook his head. "Let's go in. I need a bed, me. I'll tell them we're eighteen. If they query it, give them an extra fifty. That'll convince them."

The SPACE campaigners had heard from Patrick Finch. The hated scientist told them that he'd been affected by the death of the demonstrator. He felt that his work was not worth such sacrifices. He said his resolve had been weakened by events. He promised that, if they put him in touch with Maynard Litzoff, if some pictures removed illegally from the clinic were returned and not released to the press, he would not pursue his cloning research. As a gesture of goodwill, he would not press charges against the SPACE activists arrested on Monday night and he would try to persuade the police to be lenient. Also, he wouldn't replace the surveillance cameras above the walls of the clinic – which would save the protesters the bother of stoning them.

If anyone at the Save People and Animals from Cloning Experiments protest knew where Maynard was, they would have been celebrating victory. But not even the recently released Tadpole or Gaia Queen could guess where he had gone.

*

The lights of the city centre made sure that the hotel room was never truly dark. Jordan lay on his back and stared at the unfamiliar colours on the ceiling. Without his glasses, they were fuzzy. "I'll tell you what'd be best," he said quietly.

"What's that?" Maynard asked from the twin bed. He was also lying down but he was still fully clothed and wide awake.

"A live press conference. We could do a lot of damage with the chimp pictures – and Dad's banned experiment. Hey. . ."

"What?"

"You could've brought photos of mutants with you. That would've created even more damage."

Maynard smiled to himself in the dark. "It'd be a bit odd if I produced pictures of clones before human cloning had been tried. But, yeah, I wish I had as well now. When I came, though, the plan was to give reproductive cloning research a push in the right direction, not to stop it. I didn't need photographic evidence."

"Oh well. We'll make do with what we've got," Jordan muttered. "If we produce it live on telly, no one can fiddle with it afterwards, or suppress it altogether."

"Mmm. And how do you organize that?"

"I don't know. Not a clue. I bet SPACE would set it up, no problem."

Sadly, Maynard said, "We can't go back there. The police would be watching for us. And the people in the camp didn't use phones in case the police were listening in."

177

"You're from 2152. You must be able. . ."

"How do you know that?"

"What?"

"How do you know I'm from 2152?" asked Maynard, sitting up against the creaky headboard.

"You said."

"No, I didn't," Maynard replied firmly.

"You must have done."

"The only way you could have known it is if you've seen my watch."

The pipe running up the wall behind Jordan's bed let out dreadful clunking noises as someone above turned on a tap.

"Are you sure you didn't say. . ."

"Certain."

"Ah."

Both boys were silent. Jordan was too ashamed to say anything and Maynard was waiting for Jordan to speak. Outside, a car horn sounded, two men were shouting at each other, and a motorbike revved loudly.

It was Maynard who cracked first. "Where is it?" he asked. "Have you got it with you?"

Jordan sighed. "If you put the light on, I'll show you."

Slowly, Jordan got up, rummaged around in his rucksack and pulled out a fistful of metallic fragments. Sheepishly and without a word, he held them out to his friend on his palm.

"But. . ." Maynard stared at the remnants in horror. "But that's my device."

"What? Your device for getting back to your own time?"

Speechless, Maynard nodded.

"Oh, shit!" Jordan closed his eyes and clutched his head in both hands. "Maynard, I'm sorry. I didn't know. . ."

Without a word, Maynard ran out of the room and down the stairs, leaving the bedroom door wide open behind him. The red light from the corridor made the gap look like a large wound.

21

Everything was being stripped slowly away from him. Yesterday morning, he had a secure home, a family and friends. Last night, he had only a couple of friends. In just one day, he had lost them both. Jordan was sitting on a rotten bed in a rotten hotel, feeling absolutely rotten. And alone. No matter how hard he tried to keep back the tears, he couldn't. At least there was no one around to see his weakness. There again, if there had been someone around, he wouldn't have been crying.

Glancing towards the closed bedroom door, he dried his eyes on a handkerchief. Then he recited quietly, "Ten and nine and. . ." When he got down to zero, he willed the door to open and Maynard to return but, no, nothing happened. Of course nothing happened.

Eventually, after countless countdowns, Jordan drifted into sleep.

Maynard stood on the ridge of the hill on Westford's western edge. In his day, the track would lead to the industrial complex of the Anti-Freeze Corporation. To his right would be two lines of lights either side of the AFC's runway. Now, there were just dark fields. Nothing. Not even reflections from ice and snow. He turned to his left and surveyed the sprawling city: the myriad house lights, the amber strings that defined the city streets, moving head-lights, the shining tower blocks, flashing neon signs. It wasn't his city. If he hadn't known that he was looking at a bygone Westford, he would not have guessed. The nuclear fusion station didn't exist at all, the fertility clinic was so stunted, he couldn't make it out from where he stood. The spectacular Leisure Dome and Protected Park should have been a bright glowing ball but here, in this time, it was a few unlit and unimaginative playing fields surrounded by soiled roads.

He'd always hoped that he would find a way to return home. He'd always hoped that the watch was not lost for ever. And while he had a hope of returning, when it was still a possibility, the prospect wasn't appealing. It was something he could do when he had had his fill of Jordan's world. Besides, it would have been a strange, thankless homecoming. If Maynard had kept to his original task of setting cloning on the right path and he had successfully eradicated the tragic curse of mutes, no one in the future would know. They would have only one history – the one that Maynard had fashioned. They would not be aware of the alternative fate that he had averted. Maynard would never have had a hero's welcome.

Beyond the city, beyond the horizon, there was the first hint of sunlight. As a new day dawned, Maynard wondered if he had been deluding himself all along. Perhaps this mission had always been a one-way trip. Perhaps he was never intended to have a future of his own. Now his watch was beyond repair and he knew for sure that he would not return, he began to yearn for home. Yes, he knew his own weather was abysmal. Yes, he loathed the way norms would live. Even if there were no mutes, he knew his future society would remain corrupt. Norms would still be intolerant, obsessed with perfection, and insufferable. Yes, he knew all that. But it was where he belonged.

By the time he walked down the hill, as alone as he'd been when he had first set foot in this archaic Westford, it was daybreak and he had decided to eliminate human cloning ruthlessly. Not just the errors but all of it. He would never benefit from this quest – and he would be its first victim – but he would remould that future society into something palatable. That would be his parting gift.

If he did nothing, he could live on in Jordan's Westford, he could enjoy its variety and individuality, but he would be tortured by his inability to go home. And he would have failed the whole of the human race. He couldn't live with that sort of responsibility so he might as well not live at all.

He no longer cared whether Lights Out became a father or not.

Having ruined the watch and his friend's only hope of returning home, the least that Jordan could do was to bring Myleene and Lights Out together. He didn't also want to ruin Maynard's only hope of being born in the first place. Jordan's guilt drove him back to school but speaking to Tim or Myleene herself was going to be tough.

He came round the corner by the school and stopped dead. Two sharp-eyed policemen were standing on either side of the gates. He'd anticipated a police presence but he hadn't expected it to be so blatant. If there had been razor wire on the walls, the place would have resembled the fortified entrance to his dad's clinic. At once, Jordan turned and ran back the way he had come.

He was convinced that the number of police outside the Finch Private Fertility Clinic would have been doubled. And every security guard would be on the lookout for him. By now his dad would have made sure a photograph of Jordan was imprinted on their brains. That's why he took an unusual route to the protesters' camp. The trees that provided cover for his escape from SPACE City also provided the protection he needed to return unseen. Keeping within the confines of the shadowy wood, Jordan shouted towards the first row of tents until a curious activist sneaked across no man's land to investigate. Jordan explained who he was and why he had to remain in hiding, and asked for Tadpole.

After a few minutes, Tadpole and Gaia Queen dashed across the field and entered the wood to speak to Jordan Finch. At once, Jordan launched into his big idea for a press conference.

Tadpole put up his hand. "Hold on. Before you get carried away. . ." He turned to Gaia Queen.

She slipped her hand into her bag and extracted a cassette recorder. "Something's cropped up. Listen. We need your help to decide if it's genuine."

They all sat down on a fallen log while Gaia Queen played the tape. Jordan recognized his dad's voice instantly. Because of the poor quality of the recording, it took a few seconds more to recognize the tone. Claiming that he'd been saddened by the death of a demonstrator, Patrick Finch offered to abandon his ambition to clone humans in exchange for Maynard Litzoff and the return of the file on the chimpanzee post-mortem. There was an implication that he'd want Jordan back as well, but he was too proud to admit to strangers that his son was missing.

As soon as Gaia Queen hit the "stop" button, Jordan said bluntly, "He's bluffing. I can hear it in his voice."

"What? Are you sure?"

Jordan nodded. "Give him what he wants and he'll just carry on. Even if he stopped cloning here, he'd do it abroad. Maybe that's why he said it. Here, he might concentrate on normal fertility treatments and endocrine disrupters."

"What're they?" Tadpole asked.

As quickly as he could, Jordan explained falling sperm counts and what had happened since they had confiscated some of Fairway's experimental animals. Then he went back to his plan to provoke an outrage with the monkey pictures, unveil the shaky start of the Finch Fertility Clinic and reveal his dad's unlawful history at a live press conference. "Can you organize it?" he asked Gaia Queen and Tadpole.

Still smarting over Patrick Finch's deceitful offer, they looked at each other for a moment and then together said, "Yes."

"Good."

"By the way," Gaia Queen asked, "where's Space Cadet?"

Jordan shrugged. "I'm sorry. I don't know."

184

She sighed sadly.

Feeling sympathy for her, Jordan added, "He went off to do something last night." He wondered if he'd acquired his ability to lie convincingly from his dad's genes. "I haven't seen him since."

Gaia Queen's voice was subdued. "Will this work on endo . . . things mean your dad won't use lab animals any more?"

"No. He'll still do plenty of that. He's got to test chemicals on animals to find out if they're endocrine disrupters. If he doesn't, he won't be able to find out what's damaging male animals – including men – and what isn't."

Gaia Queen nodded. "I see." Her quiet acceptance was somehow sinister.

"Psst!" Jordan called from the alley beside the shop.

Tim looked round, puzzled, then spotted Jordan lurking in the dim passageway. Exasperated with his friend, he asked, "What's going on with you?"

Urgently, Jordan said, "I can't. . ."

"We had the police in class today, asking all about you. The teachers've got a theory you've been kidnapped or something."

"Kidnapped? No. Course not."

"Even by your standards, this is going a bit far, Jordan."

"Sorry, but you've got to do something for me."

Tim was still thinking about what Jordan was doing rather than what he could do for Jordan. "What are you up to? Why the hush-hush, lurking-in-a-dark-alleyway, my-stuff's-too-important-to-come-to-school mystery?"

"If I wasn't scared the police might be around right now, I'd tell you everything. Honest. But I can't be sure." He glanced up and down the passageway.

Recovering his sense of humour, Tim shook his head. "We all know you're taking a GCSE in espionage but this is taking the practical a bit far. How am I supposed to get through science project work if you don't do it for me?"

"Listen," Jordan replied, "this is vital."

"Are you trailing a criminal mastermind with an umbrella that fires nuclear missiles?"

Impatiently, Jordan said, "I'm not joking. You've got to help."

Persuaded by Jordan's expression to be serious again, Tim asked, "What do you want me to do?"

"I want you to go to a nightclub. The Slippery Slope."

"Now?" The grin came back as Tim glanced at his watch.

"When it's open."

"Why?" Before Tim got an answer, he put up his hand. "Don't say it. I bet you can't tell me. It's top secret."

"That's right. Just take Anita and Myleene. All right? You've got to take Myleene. That's the vital bit."

"Jordan. . ."

"It's not much to ask, is it? It's not like I'm asking you to go somewhere embarrassing."

"It's not as easy as you think at the moment. Their mum's grounded them big style and they're spending all their time pulling each other's hair out and screaming at one another."

"Really?" Jordan let out a weary breath. "Well, it doesn't have to be straight away, I suppose. When they've cooled off a bit, take them. Especially Myleene. Got it?"

"OK."

"OK's not enough. Promise."

"Yeah. I promise," Tim said with a tired groan.

"Thanks."

"I suppose you're off on a mission to save the world now."

"Something like that."

"Jordan," Tim called after him, "your mum and dad are. . ." He gave up. Jordan had disappeared round the corner at the end of the passage.

Jordan had been right about money. Maynard was almost knocked over in the rush when he offered fifty pounds to a group of men sleeping rough under the bridge if one of them could break into a car for him. The car was in the multi-storey car park next to the shopping centre. When Maynard's hired assistant started working on the driver's door, Maynard said quietly, "No!" He looked up and down the fifth floor nervously. No one was coming towards them. "A back door. I want to get in the back."

"You what?"

Maynard pointed. "The back door. The one behind the front."

The man shrugged. Making it clear that he thought Maynard was mad, he muttered, "Up to you, I suppose."

A few minutes later, Maynard was fifty pounds lighter, lying flat out between the seats, making himself as small and invisible as possible, and he was drenched in sweat.

Half an hour later, Gwen Finch removed her shopping from the boot and left the empty car in the garage. Except that the car was not quite empty.

22

Patrick and Gwen were halfway through dinner when the young man burst in, waving a bread knife that he'd taken from the kitchen. In shock, both of them got to their feet, banging into the table and spilling their drinks. Gwen dropped her fork to the floor. "How did you. . .?" she shouted.

"It doesn't matter," Maynard retorted. "Let's not have any trouble. Stay exactly where you are. Sit down. Push your knives and forks into the middle of the table. I wouldn't want to. . ." He glanced at the vicious knife in his hand.

"What do you want?" Patrick said, sinking back on to his seat. For some reason he did it very slowly as if the intruder had told him not to make any sudden movements.

"A chat," Maynard replied.

"A chat?"

"Exactly." Maynard watched them place their cutlery at arm's length. "Good."

"Who are you?" asked Gwen.

"You should have worked that out already."

"Litzoff."

"I'm going to ask you a few questions. You should think hard about your situation before you reply." Maynard almost kicked himself. What he'd just said meant nothing at all. He wanted to sound threatening but he just sounded

189

ridiculous. Neither Patrick nor Gwen responded but they did look suspicious and terrified. So, despite sounding silly, he'd achieved the desired effect. Looking at Patrick, he said, "Tell me how you intend to screen cloned embryos for abnormalities."

Patrick hesitated. "I can tell you, but I'm not sure you'll understand."

"Try me." Maynard sat down.

Clumsily, Patrick's elbow caught a glass and knocked it from the table.

"Leave it there," Maynard ordered. "Give me as much detail as you like but don't take too long. I know I won't have much time."

Patrick took a deep breath. "I've developed a DNA chip that'll give me a complete genetic profile of every cell I take from every embryo. I'll do this on a weekly basis. Embryos with simple errors – like Down's Syndrome or cystic fibrosis – will be put aside and frozen." He glared at the boy with open hostility. "Are you with me?" Seeing the young man nod, Patrick continued. "Embryos with combinations of genes that would make the baby prone to cancer, asthma or heart disease when mixed with environmental effects won't be brought to term either. Only the best will be implanted in the woman's womb. Then each foetus will be monitored regularly by ultrasound scans. Does that answer your question?" Patrick's tone made it plain that he thought he'd bamboozled this thug.

"Yes. That'll do with the diseases you know about. But how do you screen for problems when you don't know what could go wrong?"

Patrick frowned with annoyance. The boy was bright and well informed. "I use the experience I've picked up from research with animals."

"Animal foetuses that look good at thirty days can die, just like that, at thirty one – with everything apparently on track. You can't screen out problems when you don't know what you're looking for. You don't know what could go wrong till it does."

Patrick was more anxious now because a sharp mind worried him more than a sharp knife. He enjoyed a verbal scrap but only when he was the smartest person in the room. He did not relish having his intellect challenged by a mere boy, especially one with a knife in his hand. "The human gene package is even tougher than an animal's. There'll be fewer hiccups with humans than with sheep."

Maynard shook his head disapprovingly. "You've persuaded an adult skin cell to remember that it's not just a blueprint for skin but a blueprint for a whole body. That's clever but it's not the whole story, is it? I've seen your results with chimpanzees, remember, and some of the genes are refusing to reactivate. That's hardly a surprise. If a brilliant tennis player went into a coma and you woke him up after forty years, would you expect him to serve and volley as if he'd never been away, without making any mistakes? Why expect adult genes that have been switched off for years to wake up and function properly, perfectly and immediately? Of course you'll get mistakes. And it's not just IGF2R."

That did it. Patrick snapped altogether. There was something about this boy that just didn't add up. "How do you know—"

Maynard cut him off. "You're just hoping no other genes go into hibernation. Well, I'm here to break the news that you're seeing uncontrolled growth because there's plenty of other genes that your jolt of electricity isn't waking up properly. And it'll happen with humans as well."

"You don't know that. I may be *hoping*, but you're just *guessing*."

"No, I'm not," Maynard said firmly. He held Patrick's gaze so the biologist could see the conviction in his face. "I could list the relevant genes, but that would only encourage you. The faults in your method will cause a lot of still births and abortions. Babies that survive will suffer deformities, enlarged organs, immature lungs, bad livers and kidneys, immune deficiencies, breathing difficulties, mental problems, and more. They'll be mutants."

"You can't prove any of this will happen."

"More important, you can't prove it *won't*. You don't have enough facts. I'll give you one obvious example. You say you've learnt from experience with animals. But there's no IQ test for mice. How do you know their brains are working properly? Maybe they're all morons and completely mad. So, how do you know your human clones won't be mad as well? How do you know they won't have learning difficulties?" Not giving Patrick a chance to answer, Maynard became even more provocative by deliberately letting slip that he knew about the Caribbean connection. "You're going to take a wrong turn in Barbados and commit a crime against the human species."

Patrick was taken aback. He took a moment to compose himself before he responded. "I'm going to Barbados to

192

treat sterile men. That's no crime. Infertility's a devastating, silent disease. *You* should know that."

"My condition's irrelevant," Maynard argued, shuffling the bread knife from hand to hand. "The consequences of what you're going to do aren't. You won't stop when you make mutants. You – or someone else – will learn from the mistakes, try again and eventually get it right. Then, you won't stop at infertile couples either."

"I will," Patrick stated bluntly.

"No, you won't. You won't be able to stop things escalating. Imagine some parents come to you. Their one and only child has got leukaemia. She needs a bone marrow transplant from a donor but there isn't a compatible one. She's as good as dead unless she gets a donor. A clone would be a hundred per cent compatible." Maynard gazed at Patrick Finch. "What are you going to do? Cloning the daughter's not curing a fertility problem but it's saving a life. Are you going to turn this family away? No. Because you care. That's the strange thing. You care. And that's why you'll go ahead."

"A baby's a baby, not a product. It's not a medicine or a spare part for another child. If the parents only want it to save their daughter, that's not a good reason."

Gwen glanced sideways at her husband. Speaking slowly, she tried to engage Patrick and Litzoff in a long conversation. "I hate to say this but people are always having babies for the wrong reasons. Because all their friends are having kids, to give a first child a playmate, to salvage a marriage, because they feel incomplete without kids, to feel grown-up and wanted. Maybe they want to prove they

193

can do at least one thing right, or maybe someone just forgot the contraception. Whatever the reason, good or bad, when the baby arrives, it's loved and cherished."

"I know it," said Maynard. He cocked his head on one side for a couple of seconds, listening intently. Then he carried on, speaking faster and faster. "It's easy to tell me here and now you wouldn't clone the girl. But when you've got those desperate parents in front of you, it's different. It'd be the first case of cloning that's not simply fertility treatment. It'd also start the brick wall crumbling. Next, a baby dies in a road accident. Because there were complications at the birth, the mother can't have another baby. Or perhaps since the birth, she's become sterile through cancer treatment. She's going to plead with you to freeze some of her son's tissue so, when she's ready, you can clone him, raise him from the dead. You'll do it because you care. And another bit of the wall comes down. Soon you'll be making babies to order, adding genes to give each one the best start in life, all because you care."

"This is pure science fiction!" Patrick claimed. "And you're just a terrorist, sitting there, threatening us with a knife. How dare you?" This time, Patrick didn't think about how people losing an argument often resort to verbal abuse.

Maynard decided to raise the stakes. "I can get your licence taken away. I can get you expelled from APART. As soon as they hear you got cloning under way with an illegal experiment. . ."

Patrick snapped, "That's something else you got from Jordan! Barbados, now this."

At once, Gwen said, "You've taken him! Where is he? Is he safe?"

"If you set out to do the human experiments in Barbados, I'll get you struck off."

"Is he safe?" Gwen repeated.

Maynard saw another avenue opening to him. If they regarded him as a terrorist and a kidnapper, he might as well play the part. "He is for the moment," he answered, looking down menacingly at the knife. "I didn't have to hurt him much to find out what I know."

Gwen asked, "Where is he?"

"You'll get him back in one piece when you stop trying to clone people. Simple."

"Just a minute. . ." Patrick began.

Maynard was on his feet, listening to some distant noise. "You're trying to keep me talking. You should've learnt I'm no fool. I imagine I've triggered something in here and the police are on their way." His sensitive hearing had already detected the sound of several speeding cars. "I've said my piece. Think about it. Think about Jordan."

He charged through the kitchen, dropped the knife and flung open the back door. Again he flew towards the familiar cherry tree and the hedge. Protecting his face with his arms, he burst through the hedge for the second time and vanished into the night.

23

Some of the microscopic bugs in the Finches' house were still transmitting a signal. That was how Maynard had found out about Gwen's shopping trip. Now, from a safe distance, he listened to Patrick and Gwen reporting the incident to the police. Maynard recognized the Finches' version of the story but they exaggerated the danger that he'd posed. From the fierce picture they painted of him, he would not have recognized himself. He did not know how many laws he had broken. He was certain, though, that the police would want to arrest him for breaking and entering, theft, driving without a licence, trespassing, waving a bread knife in someone's face, and blackmail. He was also under suspicion of kidnapping Jordan Finch, holding him against his will and possibly injuring him. Maynard smiled to himself when he thought of his alibi: he could plead innocence on the grounds that, at the time of the crimes, he wasn't due to be born for another one hundred and thirty-three years. His smile soon faded but he consoled himself with the thought that there were probably some laws he had not yet violated.

After the police had left the house, he persevered with the increasingly weak and crackly reception to find out what impact he'd had on the Finches. He heard Gwen pleading for caution and Patrick refusing to bow to terrorism. Like

Maynard himself, Patrick clearly believed that he was on a mission and obstacles had to be brushed aside.

"This," Patrick was saying to his wife, "is where we see how supportive you really are."

Gwen retorted, "No. This is where we draw the line, Patrick. It's Jordan's safety we're talking about. You've got to call it off – at least till we get him back."

"When Litzoff gets in touch again, a promise won't be good enough for him, will it? We won't get Jordan and the chimp file back till I make a public announcement to cancel the human cloning project. He'll know it's illegal in Britain and he's got the West Indian connection out of Jordan, so he'll demand I renounce it worldwide."

"He's pretty smart."

"Yeah," Patrick replied sceptically. "Uncannily so. I can't figure him out."

"Perhaps he's got a photographic memory or something. When he got his hands on your work computer maybe he remembered. . ."

"It was like he knew more than that. I don't know."

Gwen would not let the conversation wander far away from Jordan's predicament. "So, how are you going to make the announcement?"

"Just like that, eh? You want me to abandon a lifetime's work just like that?"

"Jordan's your lifetime's work! You can't give other people the gift of a child and neglect your own. It doesn't make sense. Remember, *you care*."

Now Gwen was quoting Maynard. Perhaps he had struck the right balance between flattery and ferocity.

"I'm going to have to think about that," Patrick said. "There must be a form of words. . ."

"You've always been good at dodging round problems."

Maynard noted that Gwen did not say her husband was good at *solving* problems.

Patrick replied, "Once we've got Jordan and the file back, once this Litzoff's safely locked up, I need to be able to carry on. I'd have to say I only made the announcement under duress."

"But you *will* call a press conference?"

There was a pause before Patrick answered unwillingly. "All right."

Maynard removed his earpiece and sighed. He was disappointed but not surprised. After years of seeing off cynical correspondents and critical scientists, Patrick had cultivated a slippery surface. Maynard's plan had been worth a try but Finch was unlikely to submit now to a schoolboy.

The media smelled something very sweet in the air. Both sides of the argument were calling a press conference. It was a present from heaven. The SPACE protesters were promising a couple of amazing revelations about the Finch Private Fertility Clinic. The head of the clinic was promising an important announcement. It occurred to more than one sly hack that bringing the two sides together in one almighty conference would produce one almighty row. It would be very photogenic, very reportable. Far too juicy to resist.

They went along with SPACE's suggestion of a session in the Community Hall on Monday at five o'clock and invited Dr Finch to say his piece at a celebration of Westford's high achievers, taking place in the Community Hall at five-thirty. Then, satisfied, they sat back to wait for the fireworks.

During the day, the place was filled with light, noise and people. Now, darkness crept along the quiet corridors and slipped into each unused room, making the building cold and sinister. Sitting before the eerie glow of a computer monitor, Churchman logged on to the SPACE website and noticed that the group was holding a press conference locally. He made a note of the date and time. Then, reviewing his latest exchanges with Patrick Finch, his impatience and anxiety intensified.

Patrick: *For truly infertile men – no sperm and no hope of sperm in the future – cloning is a godsend, even if His earthly representatives do not like it much. A while ago we tried to take growing cells from infertile men and turn them into functioning sperm in bulls' and pigs' testes but a lot of couples could not cope with the idea on an emotional level and anyway there was a problem with transferring animal viruses into the mother and baby. Cloning is the preferred IVF method.*

It made Churchman physically sick. These days, biologists would stoop to any level for any reason. What they did was pure wickedness. They were worse than the beasts they used in their research.

Churchman: *It is also the way to churn out an army of Hitlers.*
Patrick: *That is a myth. It cannot be done. It is true that a clone would have the same genetic potential as its parent but*

it would have a different outcome. Its upbringing, environment, diet, influences and education would all be entirely different from that of its parent so the cloned child would inevitably grow into a different person. Also, conditions in the womb influence physical and mental development so the child would not necessarily think, behave or even look much like its parent. It is good that the environment would shape a clone's physique, intelligence, attitudes and ideas almost as much as its genes because it means a rogue fanatic cannot raise replicas of some nightmare character. Even if you had some living cells from Hitler, which is highly unlikely, his clones would turn out different. The nightmare remains the stuff of horror films and fiction.

Churchman was not convinced. On the Internet he'd read the work of some scientists who thought the exact opposite. They believed it *was* possible to clone an army of terrorists because they had evidence that a child's development was ruled almost entirely by genes. Finch was giving just one scientist's view, conveniently playing down the role of genes because that was less alarming. Science was like that. There was no absolute truth, or any real answers, in science. It was just a collection of views held by different scientists. And those self-styled experts made a habit of getting it wrong.

Churchman: *This thing about the effect of the outside world is a straw you are clutching at. Clones will not be unique and you know it. A clone is a copy of its parent.*
Patrick: *The body will be similar but the mind is something else. No one can clone ideas, imagination and memories.*

200

Churchman: *Anyone who chooses to be cloned must be incredibly selfish and arrogant. A man who wants his son to be a copy of himself is not satisfying the urge to have children. He is satisfying his own ego.*

Patrick: *Plainly, you have not met the desperate men who queue at my clinic. They have every right to pass their genes down the generations like they'd pass down a family heirloom.*

That was the plea for sympathy that Churchman had been expecting. Well, he had sympathy with anyone who wanted children but could not have them. His compassion was guaranteed because he was sterile himself. But he had no sympathy with those who would not accept God's will. Some people were destined to be intelligent and some were not. Some were destined to be physically strong and some were not. Some were destined to have children and some were not. All these things were meant to be. Churchman had accepted what God and nature intended for him. He despised all those whingers who would pay people like Patrick Finch to challenge God's purpose. In an angry frame of mind, he typed his next message.

Churchman: *Are they as desperate as someone who would kidnap your son to stop your evil work?*

Huddled together in front of the destination computer, Gwen and Patrick read the new message and looked blankly at each other. "Now, how do you suppose he knows about Jordan?" asked Gwen. The police had kept his disappearance out of the news.

Patrick shrugged.

"Your Churchman has got to be quite close to Jordan himself," Gwen concluded.

Patrick agreed. "So it seems."

"He sounds unbalanced to me. Are you sure he's safe?"

"No. I don't even know who he – or she – is."

"He," Gwen said with certainty. " A woman wouldn't write like that. Anyway," she added, "I think you should stop this little interchange. I know you're keen to defend everything you do but you're just encouraging him. He'll get more neurotic, not less, if you carry on e-mailing."

"You've probably got a point. I'll ignore him from now on."

"Good." She walked away from the computer and went to phone the police yet again to find out if they had any news of Jordan.

This time, there was no reply. Fuming, making no attempt at a proper shut-down, Churchman hit the computer's off button with unnecessary force. He had always hated being ignored. He hated it as much as he hated blasphemy. It was time to stop e-mailing Finch and do something that no one could ignore.

24

Outside the hotel, before mounting the cracked steps up to the door, Jordan looked along the street in both directions to see if anyone was watching. It was the action of a boy who was about to do something wrong. Opposite, a girl was leaning out of her bedroom window, taking a drag on a cigarette and blowing the smoke into the night air. She was being careful to hold the burning cigarette outside, probably to keep it secret from her parents. A woman who seemed to be late for something was desperately trying to flag down a taxi. A cyclist was looking in annoyance at a flat back tyre. Nothing unusual. Jordan slipped inside.

Maynard had paid in advance for a few nights so Jordan could lay low in the grubby hotel until the press conference. He also hoped that Maynard would reappear but, so far, there was no sign of him. Since seeing the wreckage of his watch, Maynard was probably brooding on his own and Jordan could not blame him. He'd come back to save the human race and Jordan had repaid him by burning the bridge that linked him to home. Jordan felt dreadful. And as the date with the press drew closer, he also felt more lonely and less bold by the hour.

His takeaway tasted bland. He wondered whether a final meal before an execution tasted dull or fantastic. Was it simply wasteful or a last chance to savour life? Jordan would never know because no one was beheaded for treason any more.

Maynard didn't blame Jordan for destroying his watch. After all, Jordan wouldn't have known its significance when scientific curiosity got the better of him. He'd inherited inquisitiveness from his father, no doubt, and was quite unable to resist tampering with a mysterious device. Even so, Maynard could not yet bring himself to return to the hotel, where he assumed Jordan would be staying, and face the boy who had settled his fate.

The first brick bounced off the toughened glass of the front window. The second came through it with the force of a depleted uranium missile. Patrick and Gwen leapt back. The brick was followed rapidly by a flaming milk bottle. The petrol scattered over the carpet, Patrick's trousers and the two armchairs where the Finches had been relaxing. At once, flame followed the fuel. In an instant, the front room danced with yellow.

After numerous arson attacks, all of the Finches' rooms with an outside window had been fitted with a sprinkler system. Within a couple of seconds, the sprinklers were activated and, with a sizzling noise, a fine spray of water dowsed the flames before any great damage had been done. Not even Patrick's legs were harmed. He was more shocked than burnt.

Seeing that her husband was unhurt, Gwen dashed to the broken window and looked out into the street. She saw two men in balaclavas retreating rapidly. She assumed that one of them was Maynard Litzoff but she was wrong.

Neither Gwen nor Patrick knew that Anti Clone had two brothers who were not going to let their sister's death go unanswered. As Patrick's press announcement drew closer, his enemies were multiplying and getting bolder by the hour.

What had failed so far? Reason, blackmail threats and a counterfeit kidnap. What had succeeded? Nothing. Patrick Finch had called off his trip to Barbados but it was a postponement rather than a cancellation. On the road to reproductive human cloning, Patrick had simply stalled for a short while. He had no intention of turning round and going back.

And then there were other biologists and other countries. How could Maynard stop them all? His recent pledge to eliminate the scourge of cloning was already looking shaky. It fell somewhere between improbable and impossible. Maynard could see only one option with an outside chance of success. He headed for The Slippery Slope where, in return for another week's unpaid work by Alex Litzoff, Maynard would receive a fake British passport and driving licence under a different name. While he waited for the counterfeiter to complete the intricate work, he laid low with Lights Out in his rudimentary flat and dined on toasted sandwiches. No longer in need of his receiver, Maynard spent his time making a few alterations to the earpiece and amplifier, then he gave it to Lights Out. "It's a hearing aid now," he said in a loud voice and pointed to his ear. "Yours."

Lights Out beamed. Everyone seemed to want to give

him presents. A job, somewhere to live, a hearing aid, papers and, of course, a sandwich toaster. If only he could see Myleene again, he would be in heaven.

The morning sun found a crack between the heavy curtains and slotted a shaft of light into the bedroom where Jordan lay in a tangle of sheets. It was Monday, the day of the press conference, and he was instantly on edge. He strapped on his watch and at once calculated the time until his act of betrayal.

The hotel's full English breakfast swam in an ocean of partly congealed fat that could clog arteries and provoke an instant heart attack. The breakfast would keep him going all day but Jordan couldn't face it this morning. His stomach was churning already. Under the window, the radiator was gurgling at full volume as if it too was suffering a bad case of indigestion.

Jordan admired Maynard. He'd travelled a long way from home alone and he didn't seem to need anyone else. Jordan was nowhere near as independent. He hated being by himself. He missed his mates at school, his home, his bed. He would even admit that he missed his parents and home cooking. He didn't know if he could survive on his own. He needed friends and family. He needed his dad and loathed him at the same time. Before the press conference, Jordan wanted to see his mum, the twins, Tim, and Maynard. He wanted their approval. He would get it from his friends but not from his mum, of course. She would never sanction anything that would hurt Patrick because she was always, *always* on his side.

If Jordan knew exactly what his mum, the twins, Tim, and Maynard would say, why did he feel the need to consult them? If he knew what they would tell him, a reunion was surely pointless. To Jordan, it was both pointless and crucial. Without that contact, he felt empty and exposed. Yet meeting anyone was far too dangerous. He had to remain in hiding until the very last moment. He would have to go to the press conference as a scared and vulnerable boy. Alone.

He lounged on his bed, resting on an elbow, with three sheets of paper in front of him. His scrawled notes were the fifth version of his statement about his dad's experiments, both lawful and criminal. Jordan still wasn't satisfied with the content or tone or anything, but doubted that he could ever express it better. Reluctantly he was learning his lines.

Without a countdown, without warning, Maynard walked into the hotel room.

Jordan jumped up from his bed and only just stopped himself from hugging his friend. "Maynard! I . . . er. . ."

"What?"

"Where've you been?"

"With Lights Out."

"Ah," Jordan said, recovering his composure. "Is he OK?"

"He's better than OK. He just wishes Myleene . . . you know."

"Tim says he'll take her to the Slippery Slope as soon as he can."

Maynard nodded but, surprising Jordan, he didn't show any enthusiasm for the reunion.

"And what about you?" Jordan asked.

"Me?"

"Are *you* OK?"

Maynard shrugged as if his feelings were immaterial.

Staring at the floor, Jordan said, "Maynard, I'm sorry . . . really sorry . . . about your watch. I . . . I haven't got an excuse."

Maynard sighed. "Perhaps I was always foolish to think I'd get out of this, so it doesn't matter."

"I feel so guilty."

"It's not your fault. Like you said, you didn't know what the watch did."

Jordan dared to look up from the stained carpet and into Maynard's face. "When you arrived and there I was, blocking your way, why didn't you just go back?"

Maynard smiled wryly. "I tried. As soon as you saw me, I made for the doorway but it doesn't stay open for long. I only missed it by a second or two. Then, you didn't exactly give me time to reset the watch. Besides, I'd made it to the right place. I didn't really want to go back. I just wanted to get away from you."

"And now I've broken it." Jordan slumped down on to the edge of one of the beds and hung his head again.

Maynard took a deep breath. "Maybe it was always meant to be, like Lights Out and Myleene."

"But I still feel really bad about it." He glanced at his bag where the scraps were stored. "I've trapped you here."

Trying to sound cheerful, Maynard answered, "There are worse places to be."

"I'm sorry, but there's something else. This is a bit much,

a bit insensitive, I know, but I've got to ask. How's it powered?"

"You've got a state-of-the-art nuclear microbattery in your bag."

"Wow. Is that dangerous?"

"No. It's clean nuclear fusion."

"Amazing. That's a lot of technology to power a watch. What's wrong with good old-fashioned sunlight?"

"It's a special device, remember. Or it was. It had to power more than a watch and a body sensor."

Jordan nodded.

"As the woman who made it said, it's got to part the sea of time. That takes a lot of energy."

"When I wore it, the reading came up, *Met Con: 1*. What does that mean?"

"Don't panic. It means your metabolic condition's good. You haven't got anything to worry about."

Eager to change the subject, Jordan said, "I decided to go ahead. I've organized a press conference – at least SPACE has. Today at five." He looked again at his watch. The day had become one extended countdown.

"That'll be . . . interesting," Maynard replied.

"Very."

"And dangerous for you."

Jordan looked up at him. "You make it sound like you're not coming."

"I can't," said Maynard. "I only came to tell you I'm leaving."

Jordan frowned with disappointment. "Leaving? Where are you going?"

"Abroad."

"Abroad? That's a big place. Where abroad?"

"Barbados."

"How do you know about Barbados?" Jordan exclaimed.

"I saw it on a map."

"Yeah. And it's a total coincidence my dad's got a place there. What's the plan?"

"I think I shouldn't distract you from your own tactic. That way, you give it your best shot and don't worry about me."

So, at least Jordan would have Maynard's blessing. That would have to do. "Aren't you going to say any more?"

"This confrontation with the press won't do your family much good and families are so important here. Are you sure you want to go through with it?"

"All families have their little arguments."

"Little? I may not know much about your world but I suspect the little arguments aren't usually played out in front of the media."

"What choice have I got?" Jordan shrugged. "Anyway, I meant, aren't you going to say any more about *your* plan."

Maynard shook his head.

Judging by Maynard's expression, Jordan guessed that he was ashamed of his scheme, possibly even appalled by it. "Are you coming back?" he asked. "Will I see you again?"

"I don't know. It depends how successful we both are."

Jordan was silent for a few seconds. "Where you come from, how do people say goodbye?"

Maynard smiled. "We don't. It's too . . . final." Before he walked back out of the door, he said, "By the way, they think I've kidnapped you. They think I'm forcing you to speak against your father." He paused and then added, "No goodbye but good luck."

Jordan nodded. "Yeah. You too."

Only the alien noises of the street encroached on the depressingly empty room. Maynard's visit had comforted Jordan more than it had unsettled him because Maynard hadn't ridiculed his plan to face the press. Also, Maynard really didn't seem to bear him a grudge over the mangled watch. To occupy himself for a while, Jordan got out the bits of the mechanism and placed the nuclear microbattery carefully in his right palm. He was utterly intrigued by it. He was holding a piece of the future. He was looking at the future. He could learn such a lot about clean energy by dismantling it and he vowed that, once his life had returned to normal, that was exactly what he would do. He would allow nothing – nothing at all – to stop him.

At that moment, his spine tingling, Jordan knew precisely what his dad had experienced when he'd first held Sarah's lamb. That feeble intriguing animal was Patrick Finch's bit of the future and he too was compelled to see it through to a conclusion. Nothing would stop him either.

25

South of the shopping centre, Main Street split into two and the Community Hall was built in the fork between the two highways out of the city. Its entrance at the junction was narrow but it soon widened as the two roads diverged. From a distance, Main Street seemed to be on a collision course with the old building. Its concrete darkened by years of exhaust pollution, the hall appeared to swallow the road and its heavy traffic.

It was a quarter to five and several vans and cars were parked lopsidedly, partly on the pavement, partly in the road, by the sides of the building. Several people were chatting to each other as they lugged equipment inside. A traffic warden was strolling past, jotting down registration numbers.

Three of the vehicles were police cars. That wasn't a serious police presence. Perhaps the authorities weren't anticipating a troublesome incident. The officers who were on duty were probably looking for Maynard because of his known association with SPACE. It was less likely that they were expecting Jordan to walk in voluntarily. At least, that's what Jordan hoped as he hung back by a side-street, discreetly watching the comings and goings. His faced creased as he thought he recognized a smartly dressed man entering the block but the sighting was too brief and distant for

212

Jordan to be sure. With a suit and tie, he certainly didn't look like a typical SPACE activist. Perhaps he was a spy from the Finch Private Fertility Clinic.

Jordan jumped when Tadpole, Gaia Queen and two young men he hadn't seen before came up behind him. "Ah, you're here," Tadpole said as if there was some doubt that Jordan would keep his word.

"Of course." He had agreed to meet the SPACE campaigners on the corner, just before five o'clock, and they had agreed to smuggle him safely into the Community Hall.

"Are you ready?"

"As ready as I'll ever be."

"Well, you're going to feel a bit daft but if you don't want to be identified till you're in there. . ." Gaia Queen produced a blond wig.

"And if you take your glasses off, that's it," Tadpole added. "Simple. If the police are keeping an eye open for you, they'll be homing in on dark hair and glasses. If you're blond and no glasses, they won't bother with you."

Jordan let out a long breath. "OK."

Gaia Queen was right. He felt utterly and completely foolish. And he imagined that his ridiculous new hairstyle looked like an obvious disguise. He imagined it attracting rather than diverting attention but the SPACE group assured him that he looked fine, perfectly natural.

"And Jordan?" Tadpole said with embarrassed awkwardness.

"Yes?"

"We . . . er. . . We thought you'd be just like your father.

213

We misjudged you. Sorry." He dropped his cigarette butt and screwed it into the pavement with his shoe.

A wry expression appeared on Jordan's face. "Not so much of a bastard after all, eh?"

"No. Definitely not."

Even the quiet and enigmatic Gaia Queen nodded enthusiastically. "You're a treasure for doing this. Totally."

"The thing is," Jordan replied, "my father's intentions are . . . brilliant. He really cares about people. That's what you forget. It's just that. . . Never mind."

Changing mood abruptly, Gaia Queen murmured, "He doesn't care about animals."

Jordan glanced askance at her. If Gaia Queen had fangs she kept them hidden but her hushed words dripped venom.

"Come on, folks," Tadpole put in, looking at his watch. "We've got to get the show on the road."

When they stepped out from the side-street, Jordan had his schoolbag over his shoulder. It held only the chimpanzee file but to Jordan it felt as heavy as lead. The two young men – who turned out to be the brothers of the martyred activist – walked in front, Tadpole strolled nonchalantly behind and Gaia Queen draped herself all over Jordan as they headed for the hall.

It was corny and embarrassing but it worked. They sauntered straight past the two police officers in the reception area and the other two who stood either side of the door into the large meeting room. The officers were peering around constantly, plainly on the lookout for someone but

214

they showed no interest in a blond Jordan, half obscured by a clingy girlfriend.

Inside, it was just as well that Jordan could not see much without his glasses. If he'd had a clear view of the journalists poised with laptops, notebooks and cameras, the SPACE protesters with their banners, and the rest of the audience, he might have panicked. Instead, he listened to the general muttering, the chanting, the shouting. It lessened a little when Tadpole and Gaia Queen led Jordan to the long table at the front where several bundles of microphones poked up like snake heads, ready to catch their every word. Anti Clone's brothers melted into the confusion.

In his ear, Gaia Queen said, "If I were you, I'd keep the disguise on till we're under way and live. There'll be plainclothes police in here. You don't want them dragging you out before you get going."

He was directed towards one of the chairs behind a collection of microphones. He did not so much sit down as flop into place. In front of him, the audience was a blurred uneasy sea. At least he couldn't examine individual faces, looking for telltale signs of support or malice. He couldn't look for undercover police, covert clinicians and the man he'd spotted earlier. He just waited for the tidal wave to sweep him up.

Next to him, Gaia Queen whispered in her soft squeaky voice, "Feeling all right?"

"Well. . ."

"Relax." She put a hand on his arm and squeezed. "You'll be fine."

"By the way," Jordan muttered, "I saw Maynard. He had to go, I'm afraid. He wanted me to say sorry and goodbye to you."

"Oh." Gaia Queen looked dazed and dreadfully disappointed. "I really wanted to. . ." She gazed out over the audience for several seconds and then turned back to Jordan. "Thanks for letting me know."

Jordan thought he caught sight of a tear. He felt sorry for her but, trying to put her distress out of his mind, he extracted the primate folder and his notes from his bag. He placed them in front of him, rested both arms on them defensively and wished that it had never come to this. He hated what he was about to do. Gaia Queen's hand returned to his arm again. Perhaps now she needed the reassuring contact as much as he did.

A campaigner stood, leaned forward on the table and brought the proceedings to order. Her introductory patter and bland condemnations of the Finch Private Fertility Clinic went on for ever. The audience and a restless press sat through it and waited impatiently for the promised revelations. Those in the know kept glancing at their watches and the door, willing half an hour to pass and Patrick Finch to make his entrance. Jordan felt like running away. But he didn't. He just sat rigidly in his seat.

Tadpole took over the meeting and briefly outlined recent actions against the clinic and explained why cloning was an immoral practice, whether it was done on animals or people.

Gaia Queen was nodding firmly in agreement while Tadpole denounced the use of animals in experiments.

Then she leaned towards Jordan, pointed to his blond camouflage and said very quietly in his ear, "We're live now. You can show yourself. But remember the microphones are in operation. They'll pick everything up."

Jordan nodded. He felt silly wearing a wig and he'd feel even more silly if he took it off in front of an audience with cameras recording. Instead, he ducked down under the table, whipped it off, ruffled his hair, and put his glasses on again before putting his head above the parapet.

There was a distinct murmur in the crowd as the spectators realized that one of the speakers had suddenly changed. A swell of questions rolled around the meeting room. "Who's that?" "Anyone know who he is?" "What's going on?" Several camera flashes spotlighted Jordan and he blinked as the media's attention shifted towards him.

His spectacles gave him back his vision and he scanned the room. The intimidating battalions of the press occupied the first two rows. Behind them were the massed ranks of SPACE supporters and the public. His heart raced as he focused on them and they focused on him. Jordan couldn't spot anyone he knew from the clinic so perhaps his dad wasn't aware of the press conference. It wouldn't be long before he did, of course. At least no one had jumped up and begun to clamber towards the table to arrest Jordan. He noted that SPACE had positioned six heavies, including Anti Clone's brothers, at either side of the room in an attempt to stop anyone rushing the speakers. Four rows away sat the well dressed man Jordan had seen earlier. It was Mr Ricketts from his school. Jordan was taken aback but he supposed it was natural for an RE teacher to take an interest in the ethics of human cloning. After all, a couple of rows further back there was a vicar in a dog collar. In school, Mr Ricketts was known to be a deeply religious man and his presence made the occasion even more nerve-wracking for Jordan. Like Gaia Queen, Jordan wished that Maynard were sitting alongside him.

Jordan listened to Tadpole for a while. He could tell where the SPACE spokesman was heading. He was talking about the appallingly cruel experiments carried out on primates and the near certainty that, if cloning went grotesquely wrong with chimpanzees, it would be catastrophic for humans as well. Any moment now, Jordan would have his cue to address the slavering reporters.

Mouth open, Gwen stared at the TV screen. The local news programme was featuring an anti-cloning rally of some sort and there, among the SPACE activists, sat her son, looking pale, uncomfortable and concerned. As his mother, she recognized the signs at once. Jordan's sickly expression told her with certainty that he did not want to do whatever he was about to do.

She picked up the phone and feverishly dialled Patrick's work number. "It's Gwen," she shouted at his secretary, "and it's urgent. Put me straight through to him, will you? Whatever he's doing."

After a few seconds, the familiar voice said, "Hello, Gwen. What's up?"

"It's Jordan."

"What?"

"He's on the telly!"

Patrick cried in shock, "He's what?"

"It's a SPACE meeting. At the Community Hall."

"The Community Hall? But I'm about to go there."

"Well, don't hang about. Get down there now! Something's not right about him. That Litzoff's probably forced him into it. I bet it's a condition to get him released. Say these things or you won't be going home. There's a rough-looking girl next to him. She's got his arm pinned down and I wouldn't be surprised if she's holding a gun or something in her other hand. I can't see it because she's keeping it under the table. Litzoff and SPACE, they're just a bunch of terrorist thugs."

"This is a stunt too far! They better not have hurt him."

"Just get down there, Patrick," Gwen said, making her own demands.

"If it's SPACE, I'll be eaten alive."

"So? This is Jordan," Gwen replied. "I'll see you there." She slammed down the phone.

Tadpole glanced across at Jordan and, with a great flourish, announced, "I'd like to introduce you to Jordan Finch who is *very* well placed to fill in the details on his *father's* experiments on monkeys." Having stressed the important words, Tadpole sat down with a smile, his coup complete.

Jordan felt Gaia Queen's grip on his arm tighten and then loosen completely.

The astonished gathering had absorbed Tadpole's words and was clamouring for quotes. A female voice boomed out, "Are you really Finch's son?"

Jordan legs were too wobbly to stand. He froze in his chair. "Er. . ." He let out a nervous cough and answered, "Yes."

"Are you part of SPACE?"

"Does Finch know you're here?"

A man with a notebook, right in front of Jordan, yelled, "What do you think of your dad's work?"

Tadpole stood up again and called for quiet. Suddenly, he was presiding over barely controlled pandemonium. "Come on. If we're going to hear what Jordan's got to say, let's give him the chance. *Please*."

After another minute, an edgy calm was restored and Jordan cleared his throat again. Several cameras flashed and Jordan did his best to ignore the fact that he was the centre of attention. Without standing, he leaned over the desk towards the microphones. Keeping his eyes fixed on his notes, he read, "I wish I wasn't here. I wish I didn't have to do this but I don't believe cloning is right. I don't believe scientists like my dad are ready to do it even if it was a good thing. There are too many unknowns and it's too risky. The trouble is, we hear about successes like Dolly the sheep without hearing about the hundreds of failures that went before." He looked up to find an almost silent room. At last something had captured the imagination of the assembled journalists. Jordan didn't know that a good few of them were licking their lips in anticipation of the father/son showdown to come. "Cloning's easy to do but very hard to get right. I want to show you some photographs of the latest cloned chimpanzee at the Finch Private Fertility Clinic." As he opened the file, there was a rumble of interest, a jostling for position, and a host of cameras and video recorders aiming directly at him.

From along the table, Tadpole announced, "We'll be distributing these afterwards. You'll all get copies of the whole report."

"This is a young chimpanzee, despite its size," Jordan said, trying to speak clearly into the microphones. "It . . . er. . . It was born alive but was grossly enlarged and soon died." He held up the first photo, displaying the chimp's chest, abdomen and limbs, and there was a groan of disappointment. The image was not particularly striking and definitely not shocking enough to get front-page treatment. Nevertheless, Jordan continued. "Dad's. . . The clinic's screening said this animal was developing normally but it still got screwed up. The cloning process makes some genes go wrong – they don't reactivate and work properly." He exhibited the second large photograph and there was another groan. This time it signified disgust. The laboratory specimen had been opened from its ribs to its genitals and its skin peeled back. "The liver shouldn't be this big or orange. It should be more-or-less blood coloured." He showed them a close-up. "The report says this contributed to his death."

The next photograph caused another ripple of revulsion. "These intestines are blocked by too much growth, I'm afraid. As well as the liver, that might be why the poor thing died but they're not the only reasons. There's more wrong yet," Jordan read hesitantly from his script, "all because of bungled cloning."

Gaia Queen had not seen the pictures before. Every

time that Jordan dropped one back on to the tabletop, she picked it up and took a look. Horrified, the distaste on her face was extreme. Now, heartfelt tears were clearly tumbling down her cheeks.

Jordan glanced at the next photo. It showed the monkey's defective heart and lungs. "Now," he said, "when I show you this, remember my dad's clinic is going to do it next with a human being. And remember, this lab monkey passed the same tests that'd be used on a developing baby. It's the chimp's heart but it's so bloated, it's hardly recognizable." He stood the image up in front of his own chest. "The report says the heart chambers and blood vessels are far too big for the heart to pump blood through. It couldn't cope and just stopped. That's what killed it a few days after it was born. So," he said, daring at last to look at the rows of faces, "imagine if this was *your* baby. Imagine this was the baby you'd been desperate to have for years."

For a few seconds, the room was completely silent.

26

Jordan's final two sentences had a sobering, devastating effect on the press conference. But, a moment later, it was chaos. Every camera flashed so that the morning papers could be decorated with Jordan Finch, drained of colour and clutching a macabre close-up of the chimp's heart and immature lungs as if they were his own diseased organs. Then came an overwhelming surge of questions.

Jordan was almost bowled over by the ferocity of the crowd's reaction.

Tadpole was banging something, trying to bring the meeting to order, trying to protect Jordan. Gaia Queen wanted to congratulate Jordan but she was too distraught to utter words. Even if she had, he would not have heard her.

Gradually, the uproar died down a little. It was becoming obvious even to thick-skinned reporters that Jordan was too petrified by the explosion to answer their shouted questions. Besides, it was unlikely that he could distinguish one from another. As a boy in shock, he deserved some respect and understanding.

Jordan mouthed to Tadpole, "I've got more."

Tadpole's lips formed the word, "Sure?" His expression told Jordan that he was asking a question.

Jordan nodded.

"OK," Tadpole shouted, his voice fighting against the din. "Let's have a bit of quiet! Please. We're not taking questions because it's up to Patrick Finch to answer the questions, not us. Now, if we can proceed. . ." He waited like a patient schoolteacher. "Jordan hasn't finished his statement."

That had a definite effect. Sensing more scandal to come, they settled down quickly. The time forgotten, not one of them checked a watch now. All eyes turned back to Jordan Finch.

Almost all eyes. Jordan noticed that Mr Ricketts had his head in his hands. Trying to ignore the teacher's anguish, Jordan sniffed, swallowed and then took a gulp of air.

Ten and nine and eight and. . .

It was like the still moment in a cinema just before the vile murder. Everyone knew that the crime was coming, everyone held their breath, everyone feared it and loved it in equal measure.

"There's something else about my father and the way he began his career in cloning."

The reporters were lapping it up, filming, scribbling notes, tapping on keypads, taking photographs.

"It all started when he cloned a sheep illegally. . ."

For the second time in Jordan's life, a countdown actually worked. Every single head in the room swivelled in unison when a voice from the back of the room barked, "He's only saying that because he's been forced to. He's making it up. Jordan's been held, brainwashed, threatened." Patrick Finch had appeared in the enemy camp.

The journalists had never had it so good. They were

sandwiched between father and son. A family disagreement, an amazing story, was breaking right over their heads.

Jordan found himself clinging to the edge of the table with his clenched fists. "Have I?" he shouted back. "No one's got a gun to my head or anything."

"Maynard Litzoff—"

Jordan interrupted him. "Is not even here."

"That can't be true!" Four police officers appeared behind Patrick as he began to make his way down the side of the meeting room towards his son. "You're safe now, Jordan. You don't have to say what they told you."

"They? No one's blackmailing me. It's just me, myself."

Patrick was truly stunned, his face startled. He couldn't believe what Jordan was saying. He couldn't take it in. After all, Jordan was his son, his own flesh and blood. "You can come home now. Everything's going to be all right."

"It might be if you stop your research."

"You know I can't. . ." Patrick sighed in exasperation. "Why are you telling these ridiculous stories about me?"

"Because it's the truth, Dad. You're the one who's forcing me to do it, not Maynard or anyone else. You're the one who won't listen. If this is the only way I can make you see. . ."

The SPACE campaigners in the hall realized that the conversation was going nowhere, that Patrick Finch was not going to break down, confess that he'd been wrong all along and swear to put an end to his hateful research. A single, shouted insult soon became a full-throated roar. "SCUM, SCUM, SCUM. . ."

The cameras continued to click and flash, video recorders caught everything, microphones captured the atmosphere that was turning more hostile by the second. A policeman, putting himself between Patrick and the crowd, was grappling with a protester. From the other side of the room, Anti Clone's brothers were pushing through the pack, closing in like hungry hounds on Patrick Finch. Ever since her death, they'd carried knives, just in case such an opportunity arose.

Tadpole was calling for order but it was futile. Gaia Queen was adding her mild voice to the mantra, "SCUM, SCUM. . ." Jordan tried to say something to his dad but there was no chance of his hearing. He shrugged and gave up.

Patrick was shattered, not by the spontaneous outpouring of resentment, but by Jordan's treachery. He began to utter something but his lips stilled almost immediately. He had been wounded too deeply by Jordan to fight against the commotion.

The scuffles and racket were brought to an abrupt end by a single loud bang like a car backfiring. But it wasn't a car. It was a gunshot that stopped everyone in their tracks.

A man in the fourth row had lifted his right arm high and fired upwards. The bullet had made a small neat hole in the plasterwork of the ceiling. A few fragments like snowflakes were drifting gently down.

Patrick did not recognize the RE teacher immediately. It took a few seconds to summon his name from memory because it had been years since Patrick had had a run-in with Mr Ricketts at Jordan's school.

The chant died away instantly and the attention shifted again. This time, everyone stared at the teacher. "You know me?" he bawled at Patrick Finch, lowering his right arm to the horizontal.

Patrick nodded. "Ricketts."

"No," the teacher replied. Both of his arms were outstretched as if he were about to be crucified or worshipped. His right hand still held the gun. It was pointed at Patrick's chest. "I'm Churchman."

"You? Churchman!"

The man nodded. "And you are a servant of the devil."

To police a press conference, an armed response unit would have been completely out of the question, an absurd level of security. None of the uniformed or plain-clothed officers were carrying firearms. They were sneaking slowly through the mob towards Ricketts but could close in on him only by moving everyone either side of him.

In that pose, the teacher reminded Jordan of the first photograph of the dead chimpanzee. Outspread, ready to reveal the unpleasant truth.

"You have no respect for God and nature," Churchman spat. "God has instructed me to eliminate you."

Patrick's eyes were wild and staring, his arms beseeching. "You can't!"

"The world is better off without you."

While the police were distracted by Ricketts, Anti Clone's brothers recovered from the shock of his intervention and edged desperately towards Finch. They didn't believe for a second that a religious man would carry out his threat. They thought he must be intent on scaring the wits out of Patrick Finch but could never harm him. Pity. As aggressive as their sister, the brothers couldn't allow Finch to leave the Community Hall without roughing him up. After all, he was responsible for her death. They wanted natural justice. They wanted to see *him* in pain. That was their right.

Relishing the moment, Churchman checked his aim once more. In the silence of the press conference, his finger drew back the trigger.

"No!" The two screams were simultaneous. One came from Gwen Finch in the far doorway, the other from Jordan.

Amid the frozen assembly, there was some movement. The police still struggled to get close enough to the gunman to disarm him. Anti Clone's brothers were still converging on Patrick. Noticing that one of the young men had a knife in his hand, Gaia Queen went to intercept. She looked outwardly calm, almost serene. Tadpole put both of his hands over his mouth and nose in an expression of horror and despair.

The brothers were wrong. Ricketts was perfectly capable and very willing to fire. After all, he was God's representative and he was saving the human race from certain corruption. There was an enthusiasm about God's zealous assassin.

Patrick staggered backwards, his face questioning. He looked down at his chest and sucked in air through the wound with a dreadful rasping sound. Then his eyes rolled upward, seeing nothing but fading light. He crumpled to the floor, his shirt suddenly covered in blood, his body ripped open.

228

Churchman stood there, looking foolish. And puzzled. Uncomprehending, he glanced down at the gun in his hand. He had not fired it. It was as if divine retribution had stepped in to save him from the sin of murder and the agony of blame.

Gaia Queen stood above Patrick, trance-like. Her hand and the knife she had snatched from Anti Clone's brother were covered in the evidence of her crime. She turned to anyone who would listen and said quietly, "He was still going to use animals, you know. Even if he stopped cloning. The end of cloning wouldn't be the end of the suffering. No. Only the end of the man could stop it. Totally."

Ignoring her, Jordan knelt on the floor and cradled his dad's head. He cried, "I never wanted this! I just wanted. . ." He couldn't carry on.

"Patrick!" It was Gwen and she dropped to her husband's side, shoving Jordan aside. "Patrick!" She let out an unearthly howl. "No! Hang on, Patrick. We'll get you to hospital. You'll be OK. Really. Everything's going to be OK." She looked up and shouted, "Someone get an ambulance!"

Softly, Jordan said, "Mum. . ."

She didn't hear. She just clung to her husband.

The vicar from the audience crouched down and took her by the shoulder. "Can I be any comfort?" he asked. "If Patrick would've wanted anything, if a prayer would help. . ."

Gwen shrugged off his hand angrily and waved him away. "Leave us alone!"

Jordan looked up as the police led Gaia Queen away.

She moved eerily like a zombie. She must have known what she'd done but there was no triumph, no remorse, nothing written on her face. She was utterly, disturbingly blank.

Beyond her, the room resembled the sky on fireworks night.

27

"Well, I don't know. It seems all wrong after ... you know ... Jordan." Myleene was standing in Anita's bedroom while she spoke into her sister's mobile.

"Yeah," Tim agreed, "but it was Jordan who asked me and I've got to keep my promise."

"Why was he so keen for you and me to go to The Slippery Slope anyway?" Myleene asked, glancing down at Neat. "It's a bit of a dive."

Tim replied, "No idea. But he really, *really* wanted us to go, especially you."

At home, things had eased a little for Myleene and Neat. They could talk to each other without blowing up and their mum had almost forgiven them. At least they were allowed out late again.

Anita had gone off Tim, though. If she wasn't going to get Lights Out, she didn't want any boy for the moment. She'd already refused Tim's date. She wasn't sending Myleene to dump him, though. She'd passed the phone to her sister because Tim had insisted. He *had* to speak to Myleene, he'd told her, because of something mysterious to do with Jordan.

Myleene shrugged. "OK. Tonight. I'll come. I suppose I could use a bit of relief, a bit of letting my hair down, after being grounded and the thing with Jordan's dad."

*

In Barbados, the experiment that Patrick Finch had planned would still go ahead. The workers at the human cloning clinic were going to make the experiment a monument to Dr Finch.

Maynard didn't know how Jordan's plan had worked out. He didn't know what had happened to Patrick, but he knew that he still had an awful job to do. Heading for the Caribbean under a false name, he glanced around the noisy primitive aircraft, wondering if any of the couples on board were the clinic's first patients. The infertile couple could be on this plane or any other. They could be local to Barbados. They could be flying in from America or France or Germany or. . .

All that Maynard knew was that he was about to make their lives a complete and utter misery. Even before he put his plan into practice, even before touching down at Grantley Adams Airport, he felt guilt-ridden. As the aeroplane began its final descent, coming in low over the coastline where the placid Caribbean Sea met the wild Atlantic, Maynard should have been enchanted like everyone else on board. He should have noticed that the airport marked the point where the tourist-friendly beaches for swimming and snorkelling gave way to the rough unpredictable waves beloved by the local surfers. He was too preoccupied, though.

In the airport itself, once he'd passed through Immigration Control, Maynard went straight past the islanders selling mats woven from pandanus grass, shell jewellery, handbags and watercolours, straight past the taxi drivers. He headed directly for the car-rental company and hired a four-wheel drive. Taking Highway 7 northbound, he made for Belleplaine. Without stopping, he drove at speed alongside the rugged Atlantic. When the road turned inland and the landscape became lush, he continued the drive through the rolling hills and valleys of St Andrew. The tall impenetrable sugar cane either side of the narrow road reduced Maynard's visibility virtually to zero.

It was five-thirty. In half an hour, night would fall quickly and navigating the unlit roads would be even more difficult. He wanted to arrive at the hidden plantation house after dark but, even with enhanced night vision, he didn't relish finding it in the unmarked heartland of Barbados. Not delaying at Belleplaine, he took Highway 1 and headed for the interior of the island. He knew only that Patrick Finch had set up his clinic in an old abandoned plantation house that was off the beaten track. Somewhere between Belleplaine and Rose Hill, where Highway 1 threaded through the hills, there would be a byway that led to the converted mansion. But Maynard would not be guided by signposts. For the sake of security and privacy, Finch's clients would be picked up and driven to the clinic by a member of staff so the place itself could remain anonymous.

Maynard wished that he'd studied the location of the historic clinic more closely but, back in his own time, there didn't seem to be a need. Right now, he wished for a break in the sugar cane so that he could command a view of the countryside. He wished he'd taken a guided tour of the island by Bajan Helicopters first. From an eagle's viewpoint, he could have located the concealed clinic. But, in his haste to get the job done, he'd set off impetuously on his own. That was exactly how he liked it, but he hadn't realized he'd end up in a gigantic, unfathomable maze.

He was losing light fast. His hi-tech eyes would make up for some of what the dusk was taking away but darkness would make his search harder. Sighing, he pulled over and stopped the car to gather his thoughts. Perhaps he shouldn't be so impatient. Perhaps he should head back to Belleplaine or even Bridgetown to ask around. Perhaps there were taxi drivers who knew where the private clinic – the very private clinic – had been set up. After all, he'd have all of tomorrow's daylight to find the place and tomorrow's nightfall to sabotage its first attempt at human cloning. But Maynard didn't want to arrive too late. He couldn't afford to wait until the syringe delivered the man's genes to the woman's emptied egg, until the jolt of electricity made the cell divide, until the embryo was formed and inserted into the mother's womb. He had to intercept the process before it began. He didn't know exactly when the experiment would start so he just wanted to get to the clinic as soon as he could.

Behind him, bright in the twilight, the headlights of two cars shone in his rear-view mirror before they swept to the right and disappeared into the plantation.

Maynard's spine tingled. A lucky break at last. At once, he executed a U-turn and cruised back down the highway to the point where the sugar crop had quenched the cars' lights. And there it was. A narrow track, easily missed in the dusk, led into the sugar cane. Maynard lurched sharp left, switched off his own lights and crawled quietly into the plantation in first gear. It was like driving into a car-wash with huge roller brushes on either side. After a few hundred metres, there was no sign of the lane opening out or developing into a proper drive. And there was no sign of a mansion.

Maynard thought of all of the deliveries that would be needed to convert a great house into the Finch Private Human Cloning Clinic. There would have to be access for lots of building materials, scientific equipment and workers. Yet this track was barely wide enough for a four-wheel drive so vans and lorries would not have managed it at all. Realizing that he'd taken a wrong turn, he turned his lights back on and stopped again.

Almost at once, there was a loud thump on the side of the car. Maynard jumped so much that his seat belt locked. He looked out of the window. It was completely dark now but his genetically modified eyes gave him some vision. There was nothing but sugar plants. Then, suddenly, a face appeared on the other side of the glass. In fright, Maynard's heart rate doubled.

But the man who had popped up so scarily was now laughing at the top of his voice.

Maynard turned off his engine and wound down the window. At once, his acute hearing detected the distant throbbing bass of rap music adding to the chorus of cicadas and frogs.

The man wiped away his tears of laughter, leaned against the roof and said into the open window: "Hey, man, your face was a picture. Looked like you seen a ghost."

The car's air-conditioning had been keeping the island's

humidity at bay. The night air was stifling. Maynard was not in the mood to appreciate the prank. "I'm . . . er . . . a bit lost."

"Really!" The man turned away and boomed, "We got ourselves a tourist and he's lost! Would you believe that?"

Some way down the road, another man burst into laughter.

"Where you trying to find, man? You're way off the nearest hotel."

"No, not a hotel. I'm looking for an old plantation house that's had some work done on it recently. It's being converted into a science lab. I'm supposed to be there now."

"You took a wrong turn. You're headed to a party, up in a clearing. No rocket science here." As if to prove there was a party going on, he thrust a bottle of beer through the window. "It's on me. You deserve it for finding this place."

"Thanks," Maynard said, "but. . ."

"You can join us." He shuffled his feet. "Some dancing, liming, drinking, smoking. Know what I mean?"

"If I had more time. . ." Maynard shrugged. "Right now I've got to find this lab."

The local man turned away and shouted, "Gordon, that job you did a couple of weeks back, drivin' and that – before you smashed the car. Where was it?"

"'Bout four miles up the road – towards Rose Hill."

Maynard could just make out Gordon, tinged red by the car's rear lights. "On the left or right?" he asked.

"Right," Gordon shouted back.

Maynard held up the bottle of beer. "Thanks."

"You sure you want to go to work?" The first man spat out the word *work* as if it were a term of abuse.

Maynard smiled. "There are some things you've just got to do."

Regarding Maynard as a lost cause, he began to walk away.

"Thanks again," Maynard called after him.

"You take care," he said over his shoulder. "And take time to chill. Enjoy Barbados, you hear."

Maynard turned on the ignition and, in reverse, squeezed the car back down the track and on to Highway 1 again.

Even with directions, the turning on the right was not easy to spot. Yet, as Maynard chugged slowly along the road, keeping his eyes on the opposite side, his headlights picked it out. This time, the dark lane that divided the sugar cane was wider and rutted with recent use. As he inched along it without lights, Maynard felt more confident that he was in the right place and even more tense.

After three hundred metres, he left behind the crop and, directly in front of him, the plantation house appeared. Leading to it, there was an imposing avenue lined with overgrown royal palms. Behind the row of palms, there were acres of lawned garden with gigantic mahogany, whitewood and casuarina trees. The mansion itself had seen better days but it was still impressive. It was a three-storey house with four enormous gables and several towering chimneys. Over the arched and whitewashed porch there was a balcony with iron railings. A newly laid tarmac drive, with ornate concrete figures and vases standing at each side, ran to the majestic entrance. Plainly, the mansion had fallen into disuse and disrepair but Finch had had half of it restored. The half that remained untouched had rickety and broken windows, a fragmented drainpipe and sorry brickwork.

Reflecting the character of the island itself, security around the clinic was lax. One of the five renovated windows shone with a nightlight and the porch was lit dimly. There was no sign of closed-circuit TV cameras or padlocks. On Barbados, there was no need for drastic measures because hardly anyone knew what was going to happen in the refurbished and secluded plantation house.

Maynard jumped the car up on to the grass verge and parked it behind some palm trees where it could not easily be seen. Then, his heart thumping, he made for the decrepit part of the building. The second window frame that he tried was so rotten that he knocked out one small glass pane easily. Putting his hand inside, Maynard lifted the latch and opened the whole window. Then he grabbed hold of the sill and clambered up, accidentally pulverizing the rest of the wooden frame. Praying that the place did not have an alarm, he leapt down into an empty room that had once probably been used as a lounge. The lino on the floor was torn and filthy. The stale air inside had been baked ruthlessly during the day and it was sweltering. At once, beads of sweat appeared on Maynard's brow. The floorboards creaked alarmingly as he headed cautiously for the corridor.

Elaborate antique light fittings were attached to the

walls of the passageway but they were not connected to the mains supply. Spiders used them as anchorage points for their huge dusty webs. Making the most of his enhanced sense of direction and eyesight, brushing away the cobwebs from his face, Maynard made for the modernized wing of the great house.

Back in Belleplaine, a supervisor in the security company sighed and picked up the phone. "Guess what," he said in a jaded voice.

"Not the old plantation house again."

"The system's buzzing me like crazy."

The guard replied, "It'll probably carry on buzzing you till they fix up the rest of the building. It's geese or another green monkey got in through a bad window or door."

"Don't I know? But they pay me to keep a lookout and you to go and shoo the animals away. Easy money, really, so I shouldn't complain."

"I got half a barbecued kingfish here. Beautiful. Shame to waste it."

"All right. Get it down you, then take a couple of men, just in case."

"Yeah, those geese can turn pretty nasty when you corner them."

28

Maynard hesitated and listened. No. It was only cicadas chirping behind the skirting. He'd reached the point in the corridor where, he estimated, it joined the entrance hallway but he was faced with a barrier. Any normal human being would see only blackness but Maynard's eyes soaked up every last photon. He could just make out that the builders had screwed the door into its wooden frame so that it couldn't be opened, sealing off the refitted section of the house from the rest.

He retraced his steps, searching in the gloom for anything that he could use to prise open the door. Under his feet, there were small chunks of brick and mortar so he made crunching, scraping noises as he rummaged around. Finding an old steel pipe, he stamped on the end of it, over and over again, until it was flat. Then, armed with a crude lever, he went back to the barricade. He jammed the flattened end between the wooden door and the frame and yanked with all his strength. At first nothing happened, apart from a creaking sound and his own gasps of exertion, but as he heaved on it, the old wood began to give. He shoved more of the steel pipe into the emerging gap and tugged again. Under the pressure, the screws held firm but the door itself splintered and came loose.

Maynard put down the pipe, dragged the door open a

crack and slipped through. He closed it as best he could, in the hope that no one would notice that it had been forced. He turned round to find himself in the foyer as he'd anticipated. A nightlight glowed on the reception desk but, after the darkness of the blockaded corridor, it seemed to shine like a beacon. From the ceiling hung a fan with huge blades like a helicopter's. They revolved slowly, stirring the warm air. Helpfully, there were signs: *Waiting Room*, *Surgery* and *Research Laboratories*, they said. Immediately, Maynard made his way up the wide stairs towards the laboratories.

He was so close to achieving his goal and he knew he'd never have a better opportunity. The clinic was dormant, waiting for staff to arrive tomorrow, waiting for the first patients. He had it all to himself. It was now or never. It should be easy, he told himself. But he wasn't convinced. He had to overcome two huge obstacles, far more obstinate than any blocked doorway, and both lay within himself.

The first laboratory hummed to the sound of its airconditioner. It was refreshingly cool but Maynard couldn't see a computer so he left straight away. He found what he needed in the third lab. It too was kept comfortable by airconditioning. Perhaps without it, the computers would crash through heat exhaustion. In the corner of the room, he switched on a desk lamp, booted the computer and sat down to create a monster who would save humanity.

His brain still in turmoil, Maynard swept aside the crude twenty-first century security systems and clicked through the labyrinth of programs until he reached the heart of Finch's achievement: the experimental procedure for human cloning. This was a step-by-step list of instructions for manufacturing a child. This was where it all began. For Maynard, it was like looking at his own conception. The crude recipe to produce a boy would, after more than one hundred years of refinement, give birth to Maynard and millions like him. Right now, it was just a recipe for male mutes. It was the experimental method that he'd been sent back to correct but, at this moment, correction was the last thing on his mind.

Of course, he could delete the file altogether but that would be pointless. There would be back-up copies in Westford. No. He was going to adjust the programme in a way that wouldn't be noticed.

Maynard scanned the fine detail, looking for one particular instruction among the many. When he found what he wanted, it was only a couple of lines in a very long sequence, like a single sentence in a whole novel. With the cursor, he highlighted the lines. If he deleted them, they probably wouldn't be missed but the effect on the cloning process would be profound. In real life, a few words not said could result in years of regret. Here in the lab, the loss of two short lines could wreak a lifetime of havoc. Nine months after performing the modified procedure, the first cloned human would be grossly, utterly disfigured. The mutation would be unpredictable, though. Maynard could not risk even the remote possibility that the clone's defects might be confined to its internal organs. He needed to make sure that the baby was visibly a mute and that no amount of cosmetic alteration could conceal the fact. He had to initiate an external deformity that would not show up during screening but, at birth, would be dramatic and desperately photogenic. He had to ensure that the cloners' first creation went several steps beyond ordinary mutes.

Maynard targeted one particular gene. He intended to make it turn off and, like IGF2R, stay off during the cloning process. It would not be just the boy's tongue that was enlarged. His whole face would not know when to stop growing. The unlucky baby grown to Maynard's revised recipe would be elephantine. Swollen folds of skin would droop over his cheeks, mouth and eyes. His misshapen lips, ears and nose would be massive. It was unlikely that his bloated neck and inflated throat would ever support speech. The best the boy could hope for was an inexpressive gurgling noise. The clumps around his ears, eyes and nose would certainly destroy his hearing, sight and sense of smell. The wretched specimen would have the unerring ability to turn people's stomachs. That would be the boy's role in life.

Where Maynard had deleted one instruction, he substituted another with subtle changes, making it even less likely that his tampering would be noticed. Of course, once the mute had been born with his shocking disfigurement, the clinicians would double-check the procedure and an astute researcher might spot the alterations but by then the damage would already have been done. The first cloned baby would be so hideous that there would be worldwide uproar. Cloning would be outlawed in every country.

Satisfied he'd done what was necessary, Maynard hacked into the file's properties. He made sure that, when he saved the amended document, the total editing time, revision number, date and time would not be updated. Convinced that his interference would be undetectable, Maynard went to close the document.

Do you want to save the changes you made to HClone001?

Guilt at this act of enormous cruelty was Maynard's first obstacle. For the sake of the human race, he intended to turn one little boy into a complete ogre. Surely the entire race was worth one act of supreme wickedness. Almost certainly it was, but why did it have to be Maynard's finger poised over the return button? If the cloned boy himself had a choice, would he willingly submit to a life of public humiliation, pity and revulsion for the good of society? Maynard didn't know, but the probable answer terrified him. Chances were, that baby boy wouldn't want to be a martyr. After all, there were very few Anti Clones in this world. Most likely, he would want to have as normal a life as possible. Rather than be a monster he might well prefer *not to be born at all*. Had Maynard got any right to force him to accept the role of sacrificial lamb?

Maynard's thoughts turned to Jordan. Here was a friend who was willing to turn his own father into an exhibit for the media circus, to humiliate him in public. If Jordan could do it, Maynard should be able to do the same to an unborn child. Yet Jordan was ruining only his dad's reputation and livelihood. Maynard was playing with life itself.

And then there was Maynard's other obstacle, the other thing that stayed his finger: his desire to live. To make a mute whose very existence would put an end to human cloning required Maynard to commit suicide. It wouldn't be like using a gun or a poison. It wouldn't be violent in any way. But halting reproductive human cloning now would simply erase his life. Maynard didn't know if it would even be called suicide. He wouldn't really be killed. He just wouldn't exist any more. But, right now, with the computer's question glaring like a death sentence on the monitor, it felt like suicide.

To ensure that humanity lived, Maynard was willing to die. He'd already made that decision. Deep down, he always believed he'd been given a death sentence but he'd suppressed the feeling. Stuck in a world far from his own, though, it wasn't so difficult now to accept his fate. It wasn't so difficult to be as single-minded as Anti Clone. Yet he was still troubled, still distressed, because it was far easier for him to die than it was for the anonymous clone to live.

Do you want to save the changes you made to HClone001?

No, he didn't want to save the changes. He didn't want to poison a life. He wasn't that heartless. The computer was asking the wrong question. *Should you save the changes you made to HClone001?* He should, yes. That way, an outraged public would see the dramatic result of human cloning and demand an end to it. It took only a flick of his finger, a simple tap on a key, but he couldn't do it. He could not turn an innocent baby boy into a twisted showpiece. It was too brutal, too callous. Maynard's tormented conscience would not allow him to use a boy's life as a tool, not even for the benefit of the whole species. It was all right for Jordan to say that the good of the many outweighs the needs of the one, but that was when the one was free to make his own choice.

Gwen and Jordan Finch had to get away from relentless questions, the press, protesters and the police. They had to have time to themselves, to think and to mourn. They were holed up for a couple days in a discreet hotel in the Lake District. It was nothing like the hotel in which Jordan and Maynard had taken refuge. This one had posh reception-ists, a gym, two chefs specializing in vegetarian dishes, a health and fitness instructor, and a swimming pool. It even had two rock stars as guests, drying out after their excesses on tour. But Gwen and Jordan weren't having a holiday: they were drying out after Patrick's death, steeling them-selves for the coming funeral.

The advantage of swimming, Jordan discovered, was that no one could tell when he was weeping. But he couldn't stay in the pool all of the time. He yanked himself out, dried his face and hands on a huge fluffy towel and then put his glasses back on. He loved and hated swimming in equal measure. He loved the water and he hated having his vision reduced to a smear. He hated the embarrassment of losing track of his clothes, his friends, his locker and the way out. Most embarrassing of all, he hated his inability to distinguish the male and female changing rooms. At least future generations, with eyesight made perfect through genetics, would not have to share his embarrassment. He finished rubbing himself down and slumped into a chair. He took up his book again to keep darker thoughts at bay.

Sitting at the plastic table, her newspaper open but

unread, Gwen had been silent, thoughtful, for at least five minutes. Her eyes red from grieving, she looked at her son and asked, "What do I do now, Jordan? What do *we* do?"

"You mean, with the clinic?"

His mum nodded. "I'm the owner now. They're going to clone four infertile men because there's legally binding contracts. They've got to. After that, though, I can tell them to carry on with your dad's work or . . . anything."

Jordan put his book down. "It's a foregone conclusion, then."

"Is it?"

"You always supported Dad."

"Support isn't the same as approval, as your dad once said."

Jordan stared for a moment at his mother.

"After all these years, I can still shock you. Perhaps you weren't always paying attention to me and your dad. Perhaps you were more absorbed in yourself. Typical teenager."

Jordan shook his head and raised a sad smile. "What *are* you going to do, then?"

Without Patrick, Gwen no longer had any emotional ties to cloning. "I thought we'd make a decision together."

Right then, the two of them, sitting by a swimming pool in the middle of nowhere, shaped the future of the human race.

29
sa

In the hallway of The Finch Private Human Cloning Clinic, the first of the three security guards whispered into his mobile. "Yes, we've definitely got an intruder down here."

"Feathered or hairy?"

"The sort that forces barricaded doors open with a home-made jemmy."

The supervisor's voice changed at once. There was no hint of frivolity in his tone any more. "OK. Use extreme caution."

"Roger."

One of the other guards muttered, "Could be a genetically engineered super-intelligent monkey. They can do that sort of thing now, you know. Specially in a place like this."

"Yeah, well, let's catch him first and worry about which species he is after."

"If he's super-strong as well, we might need tranquillizer darts."

"Come on. We'll keep together and start on this floor. The surgery."

Maynard had done his best. He'd tried to scupper the cloning programme the only way he knew but he could not bring himself to make matters so much worse for a single mute.

Do you want to save the changes you made to HClone001?

He moved the mouse, clicked on No to restore Patrick Finch's original experimental procedure, and placed his head in his hands.

He'd come all this way, made his own sacrifice, for nothing. He'd failed. He was leaving Finch's research exactly as it was. Having run out of ideas, he could hope only that Jordan had been more successful.

Outside, the hills and lakes were spectacularly bleak in the drizzle. Inside, at poolside, it was warm, light and luxurious.

"That's decided then," Gwen was saying. "I tell them to abandon the cloning project and put all their resources into preventing male infertility."

"Result. Prevention's got to be better than fixing it after it's broken. You could call it the good deed project – Detection and Elimination of Endocrine Disrupters."

Gwen nodded. Then she paused before adding, "I think your dad would support that – even if he wouldn't entirely approve. After all, he'd already made a start on it."

Jordan touched his mum's hand. "Thanks. I'm sure it's for the best." Really, he knew it was for the best but he couldn't tell his mum that he'd had a sneak preview of the future.

Even if Jordan couldn't stop human cloning, even if his dad's death only delayed it and didn't eradicate it, and even if Maynard couldn't bring it to a halt in Barbados, at least the Finch Private Fertility Clinic would work towards removing the need for it. If men didn't become sterile in the first place, there'd be no good reason for widespread cloning. The technique would be relegated to the minor league of infertility treatments. Sure, it would reproduce a few children who died pitifully young, it would satisfy a few egos, it would give some sterile couples and single-sex partners a chance of having children, but it would remain a last resort, unpopular, expensive and undesirable.

It was a strange sensation. Maynard didn't know if he felt queasy because he'd botched the job. He didn't know if it was something to do with his refusal to blight one life, even for the sake of everyone else's. He didn't know if his light-headedness was something to do with uncertainty. Had he done the right thing? After all, he'd just condemned the whole race for the sake of one pathetic creature. Was his compassion misplaced? Burdened with guilt, it would have been more extraordinary if he hadn't felt sick.

The uncomfortable feeling spread. He glanced down at his fingers as if he needed the reassurance that they were still there. Both his hands and feet were deadened. His heart still pumped but he was no longer aware of it in his chest. The organ seemed to lack power like a battery coming to the end of its useful life. It engorged on blood but didn't expel it deep into his limbs and brain. Deprivation of oxygen was making him numb and nauseous. His neck, where he had always been able to feel the throb of his pulse, had become still.

With life limping rather than surging through his arteries and veins, Maynard wondered if he had come this far just to suffer a heart attack alone in the middle of a foreign island. But no. He couldn't believe it. He'd been carefully programmed before birth. The chances of his having heart disease were too small to calculate. Besides, if he were having a heart attack, he'd be suffering unbearably intense pain across his chest by now. He had no pain. Almost the opposite. He was drifting peacefully like a ship becalmed. He wasn't even scared. He just had the oddest feeling that he was slowly dissolving.

The security officer withdrew his head from the doorway smartly. "Yes," he whispered, barely audible to the other two. "He's in here. Far right corner, sitting at a computer."

"A hacker, then."

"He's got his head in his hands, like he's thinking or something."

"There's no other exit, is there?"

"No. He's cornered. He can't escape."

"How are we going to play this, boss?" the second guard asked under his breath.

"Take him by surprise. That's how. Burst in, me first, you two straight after." The chief officer took the gun from his belt. "We don't know if he's armed so I'm going to squat down, ready to fire. You two behind me. Don't worry. I'll take him out if he turns on you. All right?"

"Yes," they both said in unison.

"Ready?"

They nodded.

"On my count of three." He put up one finger, then a second. As his third finger went up, his big shoulder hit the door.

The first guard was down on his knees, his arms outstretched, gun clasped in both hands. And he was aiming at an empty chair. Behind him, his colleagues were astounded for a couple of seconds and then they both laughed.

The officer with the gun rose to his feet, his mouth open. Uncomprehending, he pointed towards the computer and spluttered, "But. . . What's going on? He *was* here. There! Right there! There's no doubt."

"How much rum punch did you have with that kingfish?"

"I tell you. He was as clear as . . . anything."

"I know what happened," one of the others said, walking towards the computer. "It's on. Someone left it like that and, for some reason, it came to life. You saw, I don't know, a screen saver or something." He put his hand on the monitor. "Yeah. It's warm. That's what happened."

"But the lamp's on."

"OK. Someone left that on as well. Won't be the first time."

The chief looked all around the laboratory, totally unwilling to admit that he was mistaken or that he'd been duped by a computer display.

"There's no one here, boss. Just us three and a TV."

"Yeah," the third guard added. "And the lab ghost. They can probably make ghosts as well these days."

His weapon still at the ready, the officer said, "I don't believe it!"

While their colleague continued to stalk an invisible intruder, the other two glanced at each other and began to giggle again.

They were not to know that Maynard Litzoff had just ceased to exist.

EPILOGUE
EPILOGUE

It was the 14th of the month so Jasmine Litzoff was walking to Westford's cemetery. She was a good-looking, long-legged girl. For as far back as anyone could remember, tallness had run in the Litzoff family. She'd inherited the trait from the genes of some long-forgotten forebear.

It was a warm spring day and the Leisure Dome was alive with kids and colour. The spring flowers made a wonderful display. Beyond it, she could see the top of the Finch Energy Centre. Jordan Finch was a local hero. Along with every other pupil, Jasmine had been told all about him at school. It was a hundred and forty years ago. Jordan had been only 25 years old, doing research at university, when he developed nuclear fusion as a clean and endless form of energy. The scientists of the day said he was years ahead of his time and he was awarded the Nobel Prize for physics. He must have been a real genius. He died poor, though. He didn't even attempt to make money from the most important invention of his century. He published his results so everyone could make cheap safe power, so no one needed to burn fossil fuels any more. They said he restored the planet's balance and saved the world from global warming single-handedly. Without his invention, some countries would have disappeared altogether under rising tides. Jasmine was taught that quite a few other

254

nations would have had crippling droughts or floods. They said Britain could have sweltered or maybe even the opposite. The experts believed that shifting ocean currents could have brought an ice age to Northern Europe. They all agreed on one thing, though. Jordan Finch had saved countless lives.

His mother and father were quite famous as well. Nowhere near as clever as Jordan, of course, but they were a really interesting family.

Jasmine wondered whether she would ever outstrip her own parents. There was no reason why not. In her body, there was a mix of her dad's and her mum's genes. Maybe one day that unique combination would give her the edge over both of them.

The largest building on the block belonged to Fairway Pharmaceuticals, famed for the best-selling sunscreen that had a certain effect on men. Jasmine's mum and dad thought that, at her age, she shouldn't know what aphrodisiac meant but of course she did. It brought a smile to her face as she walked. No wonder the sunscreen was so popular with men – and women. No wonder Fairway's profits were sky high.

She wandered past the shabby, barely used, fertility clinic. That was the work of Jordan Finch's parents. Patrick was legendary for being the first to clone a human being. The event was notable for two things. Patrick had been murdered just before the pregnancy got under way and it didn't work very well. The poor baby boy suffered all sorts of defects and didn't live for long. These days, biologists got it right. There'd been all sorts of improvements and cloning didn't produce freaks any more. But Jasmine couldn't see the point of copying people. Hardly anyone could see the point. One of me, Jasmine thought, is quite enough. One of anyone is quite enough. Besides, there were other ways of treating infertility and, anyway, there wasn't a lot of it about. Gwen Finch had made sure of that after her husband's death. OK so there were a few cranks around and they'd had themselves cloned. Jasmine shrugged. Society wouldn't be society without a few cranks. They were harmless enough.

To Jasmine, it was a great irony that the cemetery was next to the fertility clinic. It wasn't very often that birth and death came so close, but it happened now and again. Almost everyone lived a long long life but modern science could not eliminate every disease, every risk. And scientists had never developed a cure for the botulism toxin so no one was immune, especially not tiny children. Jasmine knelt by the gravestone and laid out some daffodils. For some reason, her little brother had loved plain old daffodils. Maynard had died from botulism food poisoning at the age of four.

Jasmine would have liked to have had a brother for longer but it wasn't to be. Her mum and dad were heartbroken when he died but they didn't take any cells to have him cloned. To them, and to Jasmine, it was unthinkable. There was only one Maynard and he'd gone. Nothing, not even science, could bring him back. Jasmine had already cried all of her tears on to this small patch of grass. She had no more. Now, she hummed a tune as she tidied his grave and gathered up the old, withered daffodils.

As always when she stood, her eyes caught the bronze monument to Jordan Finch. She hesitated and smiled. For some reason, she was comforted to know that Maynard and Jordan Finch were together.